THE PARK MURDERS

DI GILES BOOK 21

ANNA-MARIE MORGAN

For my mum, with love.

ALSO BY ANNA-MARIE MORGAN

1

POISON IN THE PARK

L ightning cracked overhead, illuminating a rapidly darkening sky.

Yvonne looked up. The heavens were about to open.

She and Dewi broke into a jog as they headed along the bridge across the river into Dolerw Park. Neither wore an overcoat. The day had started out sunny and hot. The sudden change was unexpected.

Behind them, sirens blared as ambulances raced from the scene. Police and paramedics checked throngs of people before ushering them away from the main car park. Panic-stricken faces betrayed the shock and terror of what had happened.

Below them, as they stood on the bridge, were the marquees erected for the Eisteddfod, the Welsh festival of literature, music, and performance arts. They headed for it as the rain began pelting down. Yvonne and Dewi ran towards the nightmare while most others beat a hasty retreat.

Paramedics in hazmat suits treated multiple victims on stretchers before transporting them to hospitals.

"You must put those on..." A hazmat-suited SOCO officer, holding a clipboard, pointed to a container with spare suits. "And don't go anywhere until we've checked that you've put them on properly."

The DI and Dewi exchanged glances.

"What are we looking at? What happened here?" Yvonne asked.

"We can't be sure yet, but we think there's been a hazardous chemical spill somewhere in the park. It made people ill. Some described a strange odour, difficulty breathing, and feeling numb in their extremities."

The DI and Dewi helped each other on with their suits, and waited for the seals to be checked by the officers with clipboards. Once given the okay, they left the marquee as the rain petered out.

Only festival stands, marquees, emergency personnel, and police tape remained on the grounds. Over the grass lay the odd coat, shoe, litter, and blue latex gloves discarded by the paramedics. All needed securing in specified hazardous waste bags.

Off to her right, the DI witnessed a park bench removed and bagged after its concrete foundations were dug up. Specialists also collected soil samples. She swallowed hard.

"Look behind you," Dewi called to her through his face mask. "Looks like the army has arrived..."

She turned to see two large trucks parking alongside the entrance to the bridge. "Wow." She frowned. "This must be serious."

The DI felt unusually lost. Emergency planning coordinators effectively took charge and implemented predetermined measures. She used her phone to capture photos and a video, then crossed the bridge with Dewi to talk to the remaining witnesses and observers at the town side of the car park. There was simply nothing else they could usefully do in the park grounds that wasn't already being taken care of by specialised officers.

Someone had wound tape around two of the cars remaining in the carpark. Yvonne snapped a photograph.

A young woman of around twenty-five stood by the wall near the park cafe, blowing her nose. She looked up, her red eyes wide, as they approached.

"Are you all right?" the DI asked, inclining her head.

The woman blew her nose again. "It's... It is just the shock... We were having such a good time."

"Did you see what happened?"

The woman shook her head, her short ponytail whipping back and forth. "All I saw was people near one tent fall about, holding their stomachs. Someone screamed, and people were rubbing their eyes and moaning in distress. I mean, I knew something had happened, but I couldn't see what. More people began falling sick right in front of my eyes. A few people went to help, but they too started having problems. And that's when loads of us moved away from where we thought the danger was. Although it was hard to tell what was going on. We knew we had to get out of there."

Yvonne nodded. "Very sensible... I'm sorry. What is your name?"

"Carrie... Carrie Jones. I live in Trehafren."

"Were you here on your own, Carrie?"

"No, I was with my friend, Anne Parks. I've been looking for her, but I can't find her anywhere. She might have left already or they may have taken her in an ambulance. She was at the beer tent getting us a drink when it all kicked off.

I haven't seen her since. I'm really worried about her. She's not answering her mobile."

The DI cast her eyes about. "Listen, it might be better for you to go home or somewhere you have friends and family. You can contact the hospitals from there if need be. I'm sure they will set up an emergency number soon for people to contact. Do you think you could give us a statement regarding what you witnessed? I don't mean now... We can take one in a day or two, when you've had time to recover."

"Yes... Of course." The woman nodded. "I don't know how much use I will be, since I don't know what happened, but I can tell you exactly what I saw."

"That would be perfect, thank you." The DI smiled. "Please get yourself somewhere safe. You can ring the hospital from there."

"I will." Carrie nodded. "Thank you."

DCI LLEWELYN LEANED against the desk at the front of the briefing room, hands in his pockets. He was in full uniform, dark hair neatly combed, tie straight; waiting patiently as a myriad of officers filed in.

Representatives of both CID and uniform were present and, unusually for morning briefings, there was little to no chatter amongst them.

Yvonne and her team took their seats near the front.

"Thanks for coming, everyone," Llewelyn began, clearing his throat. "I don't think I need to tell you why this special briefing has been called. Yesterday saw some of our worst fears coming true. Many people are still getting over the shock. I would first like to compliment all officers involved in the first response to the tragedy. Your professionalism and efficiency were a real credit to you all and helped minimise the total number of casualties." He grimaced. "We know multiple people are in a critical condition in intensive care, and several more are recovering on hospital wards. I'm sure our thoughts and prayers are with those affected and their families. It was a grim day, and not how we expected our precious Eisteddfod to go down."

He flicked to the first slide using a remote control. "This is the aftermath of what happened yesterday. As you can see, the epicentre of the suspected attack was the beer tent. The victims were mainly among the queues of people outside." He changed slides. "And this is the field... I think it speaks for itself as regards the panic that ensued around the grounds. Those closest to the epicentre began collapsing to the floor before others realised anything was wrong. People further from the tent felt tingling in their hands and eyes, along with difficulty breathing. Seventeen people required some level of emergency treatment. Seven of those were still on hospital wards this morning, and another three are in critical condition; their lives hanging in the balance. I don't need to tell you how serious this incident is. It appears to have been a targeted attack on our major cultural festival, an event our people have enjoyed since medieval times; a coming together which, until now, has always been a safe and fun celebration of all things Welsh."

"Is that the reason for the attack? Because the festival was Welsh?" an officer near the back asked. "Or was it targeted at an individual?"

"We don't know." The DCI pressed his lips together. "There's no evidence at the moment to confirm either way. It could simply have been an attack on a large gathering of people; as easily aimed at a carnival as the Eisteddfod." He changed slides once more. "SOCO took park benches, chairs, soil samples, and tent materials for testing, and hospitals have taken blood samples for analysis. I believe they have transported everything extracted to Porton Down for scientists to pinpoint the chemicals used. In the meantime, officers from Counter Terror have instructed the cordoning off of at least one local restaurant and the town cinema. We'll be expecting our colleagues in uniform to ensure members of the public do not cross those lines. Is that clear so far?"

All murmured assent.

"Good... That brings us to the press. Journalists and photographers from all over the UK have swamped us, as you will have seen on your way in this morning. Soon, these will include foreign news crews too. You are not to talk to members of the press under any circumstances. We will release all news through official press conferences only, after a careful liaison with Counter Terror and the NCA. Both the Welsh parliament and Whitehall are keeping a close eye on this one. They don't want the public frightened unnecessarily, and definitely no more scared than they already are. Until we have the results of testing, we cannot be sure exactly what happened here. There are some areas within this investigation in which we cannot be involved. However, we can begin collecting and collating the CCTV from the park and town, and go through it. We'll want everything we can lay our hands on, going back at least a month. This attack was well-planned, and the perpetrator or perpetrators likely cased the area for some time beforehand. I'd also like you to go through any footage looking at vehicle number plates, to include local ones and those from out of the area. Talk to everyone who was at the park and witnessed what happened. You can start with those who are well enough to talk to you now and move on to those who we hope will soon make a full recovery. Let's pray we do not lose anyone who is currently fighting for life in the hospitals. That would be a devastating outcome indeed."

He leaned back on the desk once more. "Is everyone clear about what needs to be done?"

All in the room murmured confirmation.

Yvonne and her team headed back to CID.

A TALE OF TWO OUTCOMES

Sixty-three-year-old Sam Harris sat upright in his hospital bed, a cannula and drip attached to the back of his right hand. The pensioner, with thinning white hair, appeared frail in blue cotton pyjamas. They had taken him to Telford in an ambulance as a precaution because of his age. He had been further out from the epicentre of the chemical event and had experienced only a mild tingling and sore eyes. The nurse informed Yvonne and Dewi that the drip was for rehydration only, as tests had shown no lasting effects from the chemical.

The DI smiled as they approached. "Pleased to see you doing well, Mr Harris."

"Oh yes, thank you." He smiled back. "It was frightening, you know," he said with a strong North-Wales accent. "I wasn't sure what was happening. I could see all these people falling about, and at first I felt nothing at all. Until I did. It was my hands, see. They went all tingly, like. And then my eyes got itchy, and I was sweating all down my back. That's when it got scary, because I didn't know what was going on, like. I thought I was going to fall down, like everybody else.

There were young ones collapsing, too. That surprised me. I thought maybe it was the heat, you know? It was very warm... But, it was some sort of spill, apparently."

"Can you tell us what was happening right before people became ill? I understand there was a queue for the beer tent?" Yvonne took a seat next to his bed and grimaced an apology to Dewi, who had to stand. She took out her notebook.

"Yes, that is correct. The beer tent was busy. The food vans were, too. There must have been at least twenty to thirty people in the queue outside the tent, and at least that number inside. I couldn't see what was happening in there. The people falling down were all on the outside. I was eating a burger on one side of the queue, which I had just bought it from a stall. I could have quite fancied a beer, mind, but I didn't like the idea of a long wait... Especially in that heat."

"I see... Did anything happen prior to people falling ill? Did anyone rush into the queue? Or did anything look suspicious or untoward around the line of people?"

He shook his head. "No... Everything looked normal to me. Those in the queue were patiently waiting, or else chatting with their friends. The illness came on suddenly, like."

"And no-one approached the queue from the side, or anything like that?"

"Not that I could see..."

"And when people began showing symptoms, what were they doing? How did it take them?"

"Well, they started holding their stomachs, and struggling to breathe. They fell to the floor, coughing and spluttering. Some people were shaking. I never seen the like of it... All this was happening before I felt any tingling in my fingers. I thought maybe there was something in the beer, like perhaps it had gone bad. That was my thoughts until I began feeling strange myself. I didn't drink the beer so, by that time, I knew it probably wasn't the alcohol."

"And what happened then?"

"The paramedics and first-aiders began arriving. Some of them had come straight from home. They were helping as many as they could, but two police officers who had been talking to the St. John's ambulance crew asked the first-aiders to hang back. They said ambulances were on the way from Shrewsbury with specialised gear. And, thankfully, the first of those arrived soon after. The officers seemed worried that whatever had made people sick would also harm first-aiders. I tell you, it was really scary. I have never been so frightened in my life. This sort of thing never happens here."

The DI nodded. "Your fear was understandable, Mr Harris." She gave a nod to Dewi before rising from the seat. "We are very glad to see you doing so well, and I hope you can soon go home to your family."

"Thank you," Sam Harris cocked his head. "So, do you think this was a terror attack, and will you find the perpetrators?"

"We don't know yet. But, if it was an attack of some sort, ourselves and the other agencies involved will pull out all the stops to bring the perpetrators to justice. For now, concentrate on getting better. We may wish to speak with you again."

"Any time, officers. Any time."

WHEN YVONNE and Dewi arrived back at the station, Callum met them in the office.

His eyes were wide and soulful, and the DI knew he was about to impart tragic news. She swallowed hard. Part of her would rather not know — the portion of her that would lie awake in the dark pondering awful realities and bad outcomes. "What is it?" Her mouth asked before she could check it. That was the official Yvonne; the responsible adult that wanted to solve all the problems and heal all wounds.

"I'm sorry, ma'am..." He ran a hand through mussed hair, his voice weary. "One of the critical patients has passed away... She was the mother of two young children."

"Oh, no..." Yvonne closed her eyes, her lips pressed hard together. It was a second or two before she opened them again. "How old are the children?"

"A boy aged seven, and a girl aged eight. The woman's name was Charlene Tudor. She was twenty-eight years old."

The DI rubbed her forehead. "How many more patients are still on the critical list?" she asked, rubbing her forehead.

"Three, ma'am. Two of them are men."

"The NCA has been in touch. They seem reluctant to say what the substance was, but they confirm its effects were consistent with a crude form of nerve gas. They say they do not know the chemical's origin, but it is being studied at Porton Down."

"Surely the hospitals need to know what they are dealing with?"

"I think they are in direct contact with hospital staff, Yvonne." He checked his notes. "There's something else..."

"Go on..."

"Charlene's husband Johnathan was with her when she fell sick. He was waiting next to the queue of people with their daughter on his shoulders. Officers who were at the festival prevented him from approaching his wife when he saw her fall ill. They understandably wanted him to keep the children safe. Paramedics helped Charlene as soon as they arrived, but she was one of the worst affected."

The DI nodded. "Thank goodness for those quick-thinking constables. We might otherwise have been dealing with dead children, too. Thank goodness it was the beer queue affected and not one of the children's rides. Though this is terrible news, either way. That poor family... I dread to think what they are going through tonight."

"I can only imagine." Callum grimaced. "But we should talk to Jonathan and get his perspective. He had an unob-structed view of what happened. He could be one of our most important witnesses."

"Have we asked him for a statement?"

"We spoke to him briefly last night, before his wife passed away, and he agreed to come in tomorrow. My guess is he will cancel that interview. This will have devastated him, and he'll be facing the challenge of breaking the awful news to the children."

"Call him later, Callum. Tell him I will go to see him when he feels up to it."

"Will do."

3

THE GRIEVING WIDOW?

The August day was sultry once again, as Yvonne and Dewi parked their vehicle in the car park near the local shop atop Treowen Hill. They were visiting the home of Jonathan Tudor and his late wife, Charlene, who had lived on the estate with their two young children.

Dewi discarded his jacket on the back seat and rolled up his shirt sleeves to air the damp patches under his arms.

The DI wore a sleeveless cotton dress, also without a coat. She had consumed most of a small bottle of water on the journey up from the station and, although only two in the afternoon, she was already feeling the need of a second shower.

They rang the bell of the two-bedroomed terraced home and waited.

Jonathan Tudor opened the door, shadows under his eyes. He yawned widely as he held the door open.

"May we come in?" Yvonne asked, her voice soft. She held up her badge. "We're officers from Newtown CID. We would like to discuss with you the tragic events in the park, and what happened to your wife."

"You'd better come in." He stepped back, still holding the door, allowing them to walk past him into the hallway. "Go on through... The children are in the garden on the swings," he said.

Yvonne exchanged glances with Dewi.

"You'll have to forgive me," he continued. "I had a restless night, as you can imagine. I think I managed an hour of sleep, if that. The living room is through the second door on your left."

"Thank you." The DI and DS sat on the three-seater sofa, with a view out over the garden where the children were chasing each other around the swings. "How are they doing?" she asked Jonathan when he joined them.

"Better than I expected." He scratched his stubble, his blonde hair appeared unbrushed, and his tee shirt creased. "I don't know what I expected, really. They cried last night, but when I checked on them afterward, they had fallen asleep. This morning they asked a lot of questions, and after lunch, they went out to play. I'm not sure it has really sunken in for them yet."

Yvonne nodded. "Children can be remarkably resilient. Their grief may come in waves. Be prepared for that... And what about yourself?" she asked, inclining her head, her eyes scouring his face. "I'm so sorry for your loss of your wife, and your children's loss of their mother."

He sat in the armchair at right angles to them. "I've been feeling a little lost. Charlene did most of the caring for the children while I worked. I have this week and next week off, then the children will go to my mother's until the school term starts."

The DI cleared her throat, struck because he had

described struggling with the tasks Charlene usually took care of, but not with missing his wife as a person. "It must be lonely for you, now?" she asked.

"Yeah, yeah... Of course it is. It was strange waking up, and she wasn't there. She would usually sing around the house. It is going to be strange here without her."

"Tell me about the park... What happened on Saturday?"

"We were so excited about the Eisteddfod. Well, it was a big thing, the event coming to Newtown. We had been looking forward to it for weeks. Charlene spoke a lot of Welsh, and the children are in Welsh streams in school. So, it was a chance for them all to show off a bit and enjoy the day. It was hot. Oh boy, it was warm. We'd been wandering around for an hour, taking it all in, and everyone wanted a drink. So I bought some cola for the children, and Charlene said she would get us adults a cold lager. I was really looking forward to a chilled pint. I waited with the kids away from the queue, so they wouldn't get trodden on by the crowd outside the tent. My wife was near the front of the line when I heard people start to murmur and call out. People began stumbling around and moaning. I didn't know what was happening, but I stood on tip-toes, looking for Charlene, and I couldn't see her. I wondered at first if she had gone into the tent. But then I spotted her, right before she fell over, holding her chest and coughing. Well, I didn't know what to do, because I couldn't leave the children. I called out for help and, as I saw two police officers heading over, shouted out to them. But I don't think they heard me. They were already responding to the horrendous scene unfolding before our eyes. They told us all to stand back. Some people who were there started looking over the casualties to see what they could do to help. At least one of those began showing symptoms themselves. It was crazy. There was barely time to make sense of it all. People went from being fine to keeling over, just like that. I thought maybe it was the heat, and I didn't think it would turn out this bad. Honestly, I thought the paramedics would sort everything out when they arrived. I tried getting to my wife when I realised things were serious, despite what the officers had said. But they pushed me back. I took the children to my mother's and went to Shrewsbury hospital to be with Charlene. She passed away in the night." He hung his head.

"I'm so sorry, Mr Tudor." Yvonne sighed, eyeing the photographs on the sideboard. There were several of Charlene playing with the children, her blonde hair flying around her head, and one of her and Jonathan on their wedding day. "It was an awful end to what should have been a happy family day out."

"Tell me about it. I still haven't got my head around it all. It is surreal; like a dream I can't wake up from."

"Do you mean a nightmare?" Her eyes scoured his face.

"Yes, exactly..." He nodded. "A nightmare."

"Did you notice anything else untoward before people became ill? Was there a surge within the crowd? Or anyone running away from the tent?"

He shook his head. "Not that I recall. I was reassuring the kids, though, so I wasn't paying close attention to the surrounding people. My children were crying. They were terrified."

"Was there anything else that stood out to you that day? Anything at all?"

"No... Nothing."

"Have victim liaison officers been in contact with you?"

"Yes, and they are coming again tomorrow. They are organising bereavement counselling."

Seven-year-old David came in from the garden. "Daddy, when is mummy coming back?"

Jonathan looked at the DI and grimaced.

Yvonne handed him her card. "We're sorry again, Mr Tudor. That is my number if you need us for anything or you remember something you think we should know. We'll leave you to talk to your children."

As she and Dewi left the home, the DI's heart lay heavy in her chest. She caught sight of eight-year-old Emily sat on the swing. She was barely moving; staring down at her feet. Yvonne suppressed the urge to run and hold her.

The DS put his hand on Yvonne's shoulder. "Come on... We had better get back."

They were almost at the car when a dark-haired young woman of around twenty-five approached them. "Are you police?"

"Yes..." The DI waited for the woman to continue.

"Sorry, I couldn't help but notice you going to the Tudor house..."

"Is something wrong?" Yvonne cocked her head.

"Well, I heard the awful news about Charlene." The woman appeared unsure whether to say anything further, like she was wrestling with herself.

"What is it?" the DI probed.

"Well, Charlene was thinking about divorcing Jonathan."

"Was she?" Yvonne frowned. "What makes you say that?"

"She told me. We used to do volunteer work at the community centre together, and we would often get talking about our families. She told me Jonathan had an affair, and that they'd been arguing."

"When was this?"

"Around six months ago."

"Did she say who the affair was with?"

"No, she didn't. I don't know whether she knew, or was simply protecting her husband, but she said she didn't know who it was with. She said it seemed like he was definitely having a fling with another woman and told me her family knew about it."

Yvonne handed the woman a card. "Please, could you call us, and leave your name and number with the station so we can contact you again if we need to? The information may be irrelevant, but we would like your details in case it is significant."

"Sure, I'll ring through later today. My name is Amy. Amy Jones."

"Thank you, Amy. Don't forget to call."

"I won't."

WHEN YVONNE and Dewi arrived back at the station, there was more bad news.

"I'm sorry to tell you this, but another of Saturday's victims has passed away." Callum ran a hand through his hair and sighed. "It was another of the critical cases. Forty-nine-year-old Tom Hawkins... He leaves his widow and four grown-up children."

The DI put her face in her hands. "My God, let us hope we do not lose more."

"Everyone is frightened. This is receiving coverage from all the major news channels in the UK."

"Well, I think we can understand why. And we don't yet know who did this, or what their motive was. No-one has claimed responsibility, and we have yet to hear from

Counter Terror or the NCA regarding the findings from Porton Down. Is it me, or is the silence deafening?"

Dai grimaced. "The silence is definitely deafening, Yvonne."

"What are they saying about the other victims, and the third critical case?"

"The third person taken to intensive care appears to be in recovery, ma'am. That, at least, is good news. All other victims are doing well or have made a full recovery. Some still have some tingling and numbness, etc, but they don't expect to lose any more people."

"Good. That is the best news so far." She nodded. "And how are we coming along with witness interviews?"

"Uniform have been busy questioning people who were in the park that day. They are keeping us informed regarding witnesses that may have vital information. They'll give us a list of the ones we should talk to. Though I expect the posh agencies will want to speak to them first," Callum said, referring to Counter Terror and the NCA.

"And the town CCTV?"

"Still being examined. Nothing has jumped out as yet."

Yvonne nodded. "Very well, please keep me informed."

"Will do."

4

FACTORY FARM

"**M**a'am..." Callum handed her a file. "We've asked a person of interest to come in this afternoon for an interview. One Hywel Owen... He was at the Eisteddfod early on the day of the attack and left around twenty minutes before the first victims began showing symptoms."

"Okay..." She frowned. "Is that the only reason we are asking him in?"

"No, Yvonne, he has an interesting history. It's all in the file, but the courts convicted him last year of setting up a cannabis farm at a rural property near Llanfair Caereinion. He came out of prison two months ago."

"I see."

"Also, while awaiting trial, he sent a threatening letter to the local councillor who had reported him for growing the stuff. And, when still only seventeen, he put weedkiller in his colleagues' tea while working at a local garage. Only small amounts, but enough to give them a sick stomach and diarrhoea. He received a conditional discharge for that offence as he insisted he did it for a joke, not realising how ill it would make his workmates. They all made a full recovery."

"Sounds like he might be dangerous to know." The DI grimaced. "Okay, Dewi and I will interview him. What time is he coming in?"

"At two o'clock, ma'am."

"Great, thank you, Callum."

Two o'clock came around too fast. The DI had not yet stopped for lunch. She thought of Tasha and smiled. Her partner would do her nut if she knew Yvonne hadn't eaten.

The DI put thoughts of her grumbling stomach to one side. She had the interview of their first suspect to conduct.

Hywel Owen sat in interview room two, holding a plastic cup of coffee between both hands. He had slicked his thinning hair over his crown, and was wearing an ill-fitting suit jacket and waistcoat over jeans. The buttons on the waistcoat were under strain. Records confirmed his age as forty-two. He eyed Yvonne and Dewi in silence as they took their seats.

Yvonne arranged her papers, giving Owen a nod. "Good afternoon, Mr Owen... Thank you for coming in. She announced the names of all present for the recording."

His brow furrowed, like he was trying to assess her character. "You told me to come in."

"So we did." She smiled. "But thank you for complying with our request."

He shrugged. "I don't want to be here. I thought I'd seen the last of your lot."

"Yes, I understand you got into trouble again last year?"

"You know I did. That's why you've called me in. You

think what happened at the Eisteddfod resulted from my vendetta against the system, don't you?"

"Did it?"

He frowned. "No, it bloody-well did not."

"I'm simply curious that you mentioned the Eisteddfod before we asked you about it." The DI sat back in her chair, perusing his record. "I can see you were first before the courts when you were seventeen. Can you tell us about that?"

He shrugged. "I was young and foolish. It was a prank gone horribly wrong."

"Care to elaborate?"

"Well, I thought I'd play a joke on the blokes I worked with. It's the sort of thing lads do when they are seventeen. I was working long hours at the village garage as a trainee mechanic. I wanted to liven things up."

"So, what did you do?"

He looked at the notes in front of her. "You know what I did. You've got it all there on the table. I can see it." He scowled.

"Yes, but I would like to hear it from you."

"As the youngest person there, I was the one who had to make the tea in an old metal pot. Well, I decided it would be funny, and my way of revenge, to put something in it that would make them blow off a lot, or shit their pants."

"What did you use?"

"Weed killer. I could easily buy it off the shelf, and I thought if I just used a few drops, it wouldn't do any harm."

"But you made your coworkers very sick."

"Well yeah, but hindsight is a wonderful thing, isn't it?"

"If you had known then what you know now, would you still have done it?"

"Well no, obviously. I got six months for it. Even after the courts agreed, I had only done it for a joke."

"So, the threat of prison is the only thing preventing you from doing it again? What about the effect it had on your colleagues?"

"They fully recovered, didn't they? All of them were fine afterwards. They went home that day with sickness and diarrhoea, and thought it was a bug. They got a few days off work." He shrugged.

"How were you found out?"

"They went to their GPs. One decided he'd like more tests done. The doctor thought someone may have poisoned his patient, and his suspicion was correct. Then they tested all the lads, and I was the only one who didn't fall sick. They examined the teapot, and they caught me. Well, I couldn't deny it, could I?"

"You stayed out of trouble for a long time after that."

"Twenty years."

"How did you get into cannabis?"

"I started having back pain. I used it for that. And then I had the idea I could grow it instead of buying it. I wasn't growing it to sell."

"The officer who arrested you, and the prosecution, believed that you would likely have sold it within months, if not arrested. You had many more plants than you could have used personally."

"Yeah, but I had no previous convictions for supply, and I hadn't started selling it. But they made me serve over half of a ten-month sentence. They should have released me after five, but I did seven."

"That's because you sent your local councillor a threatening letter from prison."

For the first time, Hywel stopped talking. He looked down at his hands.

"Why did you do that?"

"Because he was the one who shopped me."

"Did you think he would receive your letter and not do anything about it? That you would serve four months and they would let you out? After threatening to 'do him'?"

"It didn't get as far as the councillor. The prison staff who routinely checked our letters found it."

"I see..."

"Look, I've made a few mistakes in my life. Who hasn't?"

"There aren't many in society that make the sort of mistakes you did. These were all serious matters."

"I knew you lot would look at me. The minute I realised it was some sort of poisoning at the park. I thought, 'I bet they come talking to me because of my history.'"

"And you were right."

He folded his arms, eyes once more on the table.

"You were there that day."

"Along with several thousand other people." He scowled.

"You left twenty minutes before people became ill."

"Coincidence."

"Really?"

"Really. Lousy timing, that's all. I am sure if you had been standing at the gates, you'd have seen others leaving as well; not just me."

"Did *you* see people leaving?"

"There were some coming and going all the time. There always is at that sort of event."

"Have you been to other Eisteddfods?"

"No... I only went to this one because it was in Newtown. It was convenient. A few years ago, I almost went to the one in Aberystwyth, but I decided against it because I didn't want to travel that far. I had too much going on at home."

"Hmm... Clearly, you did." She raised a brow, her jibe aimed at the cannabis conviction. "You've led a risky life, Hywel. Had you never thought of playing it safe? Doing the right thing? Keeping your nose clean?"

"I thought about it... Yeah."

"The letter you sent to the councillor."

"What about it?"

She pulled it out from her sheaf of papers. "I have it here..."

His neck shrank, disappearing into his shirt.

"How were you planning to 'do him' exactly?"

"Well, I didn't have a plan, did I? I just wanted him to be afraid. I mean, with my history and my second stint in prison, I thought a letter like that would make his knees knock a bit. I meant it as a punishment, really. It wasn't something I ever thought I would actually carry out. Shame he never got it. I didn't get the satisfaction of seeing him squirm."

"When did you realise they had intercepted it?"

"When they hauled me in front of the prison governor and gave me extra sessions with my probation officer. I was gutted... Not because of the telling off, but because it hadn't gone to its intended target and had the desired effect." He sighed, pushing his hands into his trouser pockets and stretching his legs under the table. "You win some; you lose some."

"Were you involved in what happened at Dolerw Park last Saturday?"

"No."

"Was there anyone at that beer tent who had gotten under your skin for any reason?"

"If there was, I didn't see them."

"Were you at the beer tent?"

"At one point."

"Are you irritated with anyone at the moment?"

He pursed his lips.

"Present company excepted." She sighed.

"Not really..."

"So, there is someone?"

"No."

"Where did you go after you left the field?"

"I headed over the bridge and through the car park to town because I wanted a something to eat, and didn't fancy paying the kinds of prices charged by food vans at these events. I could have bought three or four lots of sandwiches for the price some of them were charging."

"Are you short of money?"

"Not exactly, no."

"Where does your money come from?"

He frowned. "I don't think that's any of your business."

"Well, it is if you are farming the whacky baccy to sell."

"I haven't done that since before I went to prison."

"How do you feed yourself?"

"I came into a small inheritance when my uncle died and they sold his house. And I had some savings that were not confiscated as proceeds of crime. I do all right, but I have to be careful. It won't last forever. I do a bit of gardening work and odd-jobbing as well, just to make sure I still have pennies rolling in. God gave me a bit of a green finger. I'm good with plants."

"I've seen the evidence," she said, pulling out a black-and-white photocopy of a photo of the cannabis he had been growing prior to his arrest eighteen months prior.

His face darkened, the furrows deepening on his brow. "Can I go now?"

"Yes, you can, but I wouldn't go too far if I were you. We may wish to speak with you again."

"WHAT DO YOU THINK?" She asked Dewi, as they walked down the corridor afterwards.

"I think we are right to monitor him. He's a slippery character; I wouldn't put much past the man. As for him committing the attack in the park? I don't know... Something tells me our Mr Owen is not sophisticated enough for that. I realise I may have to eat my words later, but I don't think he could pull it off."

"Hmm... You may be right, and I understand where you are coming from, but I think we should watch him. He evidently bears grudges and has a thirst for revenge when he feels wronged. Past behaviour being the best predictor of future behaviour, I wouldn't put the park attack past him. He could easily read up on the things he needed to know if it achieved his vengeful goals."

"I see your point..." Dewi nodded as they arrived back in CID.

Dai interrupted them, pen tucked behind his ear. "Can I tell you two about this CEO I've been looking at?" He flicked through his notepad.

"Sure..." The DI leaned her bottom against a desk. "Fire away."

"Right... There's a guy called Kamal Bronson, CEO of a company called 'Bronson Holdings'. They are a UK-based outfit, but have interests both here and abroad."

"Go on..."

"The company, as the name suggests, has a history of acquiring failing businesses on the cheap, and selling them on or liquidating their assets. There have faced court hearings in the past for draining off pension funds of businesses, and leaving their former employees with little or no money for their future."

"Kamal Bronson? That's an unusual name..." The DI frowned.

"His mother hailed from Pakistan, and his dad is Welsh, with some family in America. He lived over in America for a couple of years, apparently."

"I see..."

Dai continued. "Apparently, his company gained several pieces of land in Powys recently, and two years ago he offered to buy part of Dolerw Park in order to erect a riverside restaurant to run alongside the new complex already planned. The local press reported him as being angry when the council turned down his proposal. He had been so convinced they would agree to his plans."

"Really?" The DI cocked her head. "Dig up everything you can on Kamal Bronson. I think we should have a word with him as soon as possible. What do you think, Dewi?"

"Definitely... Dai, could you arrange for us to interview him?"

Yvonne nodded. "We can go see him at his company offices, if that is what he would prefer." She enjoyed seeing people in their own environment. It gave her a clearer picture of the person they were.

"Will do." The DC took his pen out from behind his ear. "I'll let you know when I've arranged the appointment."

5

A TALE OF TWO SOLUTIONS

Yvonne opened an email from the DCI. It requested that she go see him at the earliest opportunity. She frowned, finding it odd that Llewelyn would email her instead of popping through to see her, or catching up over a coffee as he would usually do. It must be serious, she mused.

She knocked on his door, straightening her skirt before walking in.

"Ah, Yvonne... Come in. Shut the door, would you?"

She did as she was told, his request confirming her belief this must be serious.

The DI didn't speak, waiting instead for Llewelyn to say his piece.

He took off his reading glasses, setting them down on the desk. "This is a sensitive topic, Yvonne, and I haven't been told much more than I can reveal to you, but it's about the chemical incident at the Eisteddfod."

"I see..."

He sighed. "Please, take a seat."

She did as she was told.

He stood, placing his hands in his pockets and walking to the window where he lingered, looking out over Dolerw Park. "I understand two of the victims have died..."

"Yes, sir, sadly they have."

"We're not alone on this." He turned to face her. "Counter Terror and the NCA have launched a major investigation. We are to aid them in any way we can."

"Understood, Chris."

"I can also tell you they have identified the substance involved."

"Oh?" She cocked her head.

"It was a neurological toxin, delivered in two stages."

"Two?"

"Yes." He nodded. "Each on their own would have caused no harm. The victims had to be exposed to both in order to have symptoms."

"I don't understand." She frowned. "Were people sprayed twice?"

He shook his head. "They don't think the perpetrator sprayed them. And I cannot say too much about it right now, and not really any more than I have already said. We won't be involved in looking at the chemical makeup of the substance or where it came from. That will be entirely down to the agencies. But we can continue going through CCTV footage, and identifying suspects and suspect vehicles."

"So, we won't be told about the toxin?"

He shook his head. "They don't want people frightened unnecessarily. We must identify the potential perpetrator or perpetrators as soon as possible, before they have the chance to do this somewhere else."

"Of course."

"That is all, Yvonne. Except..."

"Sir?"

"Be careful out there. And warn the team. You must immediately inform the agencies and myself if you suspect this chemical of being used elsewhere."

"Understood."

As Yvonne rejoined her team, she mused on the secrecy and apparent delicate nature of the investigation. What exactly was going on?

Dewi handed her a mug of tea. "You look bemused, ma'am."

"I am, Dewi." She pursed her lips. "They've identified the toxic substance."

"And?"

"We're not to speak of it in public. Other agencies will deal with that aspect."

"Do we know what it was?" Dewi sipped his tea.

"They do, but they are not telling us, at least not yet."

"Oooh, mysterious." He raised a brow.

"Quite... The DCI said the perpetrator delivered it in two stages. I think he meant one substance, followed by the other? Each on their own would have been harmless. But when the chemicals mixed, it created the harmful effects we saw."

"Oh, dear..." Dewi pursed his lips.

"What?"

"It would make sense..."

"What would?" She frowned.

"The neurological symptoms..."

"Come on, Dewi. Don't keep me guessing."

"The DCI already told us it was a type of nerve gas, right?"

Yvonne cast a glance around the office, checking no-one else was listening. "Keep your voice down. I don't know how much we can say, and this mustn't get out to the public at this stage. I remember... He mentioned it at the briefing. But he didn't say what it was."

"Had you heard of Kim Jong Nam?" Dewi cocked his head, hands in his trouser pockets.

She frowned. "Kim Jong Nam? Isn't he the leader of North Korea?"

"No, his brother, Kim Jong Un, is the leader of North Korea. Kim Jong Nam was a Korean dissident and the Korean leader's brother. He and his brother had fallen out, and Nam moved to America. Two women assassinated him in twenty-seventeen, in Kuala Lumpur International Airport."

"What has that got to do with our toxic substance?"

"I'm getting to it." He grinned. "Patience is a virtue..."

She chuckled. "I'll give you patience is a virtue. Come on... spill."

"Two women approached the victim at the airport from behind. Each had a cloth between their hands. First one, and then the other, of the women wiped their cloth over the mouth and nose of Kim Jong Nam. You can Google this yourself. They caught it on airport CCTV footage. Within moments, he began feeling ill and approached the airport staff, asking for help. In a matter of minutes, he became powerless and received first aid. Within twenty minutes, he was dead."

"Oh my God..."

"Yeah... The second of the two women also needed treatment. She had washed her hands immediately after attacking the victim, but still became ill. She recovered, however. Authorities prosecuted both women, who claimed during the trial that a man deceived them into carrying out the assassination by falsely informing them it was part of an internet prank. The man had them going around performing 'pranks' for a year before the actual attack. The women thought they were doing it for laughs and money on the net, but in fact, and unbeknown to them, they were in training for an assassination."

Yvonne stared at Dewi, opened-mouthed. "So each cloth had one of the two substances on it."

"Exactly." Dewi nodded. "The two reagents together made the nerve gas, believed to be Novichok or VX. Both of which are highly toxic, and usually deadly."

"Bloody hell." Yvonne swore, which was unlike her. "So, we may have had a similar situation at the Eisteddfod."

"Perhaps... I remember the papers, in twenty-seventeen, reporting the government requesting UK paramedics carry the antidote to nerve gas routinely. Maybe this attack was only a matter of time?"

"Didn't a similar event happen in Salisbury a few years back?"

The DS nodded. "It did... Russian agents allegedly tried to poison a Russian dissident."

Yvonne frowned. "So if your idea is correct, Dewi, the attacker must have exposed people to two chemicals." Yvonne said, frowning. "No-one questioned so far has described seeing an attacker. Or having a cloth rubbed on them."

"It's possible they would not have seen the attacker."

"Meaning?"

"Perhaps the perp sprayed one constituent in a different location, like a bench or car door handle, and they had it on their skin or clothing. Then, they touched or otherwise became exposed to the second agent in the park."

"Got it, of course." Yvonne nodded.

"I think the beer tent must have been where the second substance was located, or sprayed. The people who became sick must have already contacted substance one earlier on, in some other place."

"Makes sense... But why go to the trouble to distribute it as two solutions? Why not one mixture in a spray bottle?"

"Too dangerous... The person transporting the bottle would be seriously at risk of dying themselves. And so too, the person who mixed the contents of the bottle. Likely, both would be dead."

"Got you." The DI placed her hands on her hips. "Well done, Dewi, well done... It is all making sense. Llewelyn wants a tight lid on this. But if your theory is correct, it should give us a head start with identifying the perp. They have to have the means, knowledge, and motive, or connections to those with the means, to carry out this sort of attack."

"Exactly."

CHARMAINE DAVIES, sister of the late Charlene Tudor, was a single mother also living on Treowen Estate, only one housing close away from her sibling.

Although Yvonne felt it unlikely family matters motivated the chemical attack, she felt that if anyone could give her an insight into Charlene's life with her husband, it would be the sister with whom she was very close. The DI conducted the interview on her own, freeing up the rest of her team to chase other important leads in the case.

Charmaine's house was almost a replica of her sister's, though the arrangement of the decor was different. The layout of the house was the same, and they had similar taste in furniture.

The DI followed her through to the kitchen, where the sandy-haired Charmaine, her hair held back from her face by glasses pushed atop her head, put the kettle on. Two chunky mugs awaited hot water, their teabags already inserted.

"Thank you for agreeing to see me." The DI's eyes were soft with empathy. "May I begin by saying how sorry I am for your loss? This must have been a terrible shock."

Charmaine poured the water on the teabags. "You don't expect something like this." She turned to face Yvonne. "You understand you might lose a parent; that they will probably pass before you... But your sister? And because of what took place in the park? How in the world does that happen? Why did it happen? Do we even know what happened? They are not saying much about it, are they? The authorities are tight-lipped over everything. I mean, what's that all about? How are we supposed to make sense of it all?"

"It is a terrible situation all round," the DI agreed.

"And then there's her children." Charmaine finished brewing the mugs of tea and handed one to Yvonne. "What on earth do we tell Emily and David? Mummy has gone to heaven because something we're not sure about went down in the park?"

"How are the children?" Yvonne inclined her head.

"I have seen little of them, unfortunately. Jonathan seems to have shut the family away. He says they need time to grieve... Which I understand, to a degree, but I would have thought the kids would benefit from having female relatives around."

"How has he taken it? It must be difficult for him?" the DI asked, grateful for this lead on the husband.

"It's hard to tell... He doesn't say much. And, like I said, he has kept the family pretty much private since Charlene's death."

"Her passing would have devastated him..."

"You would like to think so." Charmaine frowned.

"But?"

"But I'm not sure how distraught he really is."

"What makes you say that?" Yvonne sipped her tea.

"Charlene and I were very close. We grew up in a large family. There were six of us kids, and she and I were the oldest and closest in age. While mum concentrated on the younger kids, we took care of ourselves. At one time, we were inseparable. And, as we grew older and had children of our own, we talked a lot. We were always at each other's houses. Jonathan worked late regularly, and my husband Tom does shift-work. So Charlene and I would alternate making tea for our children and have a good natter while the kids played together. We talked about, and shared, everything."

"Go on..."

"About six months ago, Charlene came to my house and said she believed Jonathan was having an affair with a woman at his work."

"What is his job?"

"He works on an industrial estate in Shrewsbury, for a company called 'Kemikal'. They supply chemicals for laboratories, schools, and so on."

"Really?" The DI's brow furrowed as she wrote it down, along with a note to ask Callum and Dai to chase up details on the company.

"And what made your sister believe Jonathan was having an affair?"

"He went off to a conference a couple of months prior to

Charmaine discussing it with me. She said he acted differently when he came back. He was distant and made late-
night phone calls after she went to bed."

"Did she hear what he said on these calls?"

"She said she listened on the stairs one time and,
hearing the endearments he was using and what he was
saying, she felt sure he was having an affair."

"Did she ask him about it?"

"She did, and he denied it. And in the end, he refused to
discuss it with her. When she mentioned it, he would walk
out of the room."

"How did she react to that?"

"She became frustrated and told me a few weeks ago
that she was thinking of leaving and taking the kids."

The DI noted everything down. "Did she tell Jonathan
this?"

Charmaine shrugged. "I don't know... She told me she
was thinking of telling him, but I don't know if she followed
through with it."

"When did she tell you she was considering it?"

"Two weeks ago."

"Really?"

"Yes."

"I see..." Yvonne paused her note-taking to ponder this.

"I think she was worried about telling him." Charmaine
set her mug down on the table.

"Why?"

"She didn't know how he would react... Especially about
the children."

"Did he ever hurt her? Or the children?"

The woman shook her head. "No, I don't believe so. I
think she would have told me if he had. And there was
never any bruising on her. I doubt there was an issue with

domestic violence. It was more about his being distant. They weren't communicating properly, and his behaviour convinced Charlene there was another woman."

"Have you seen him at all since she died?"

"Once... He came round to ask me if I would look after the children. He said he had to go into work."

The DI frowned. "But surely he would be on compassionate leave?"

"He is, as far as I know, but they needed something urgent sorting out, and he was the only one that could do it. That's what he told me, anyway?"

"You look sceptical..."

"Well, I suspected he was going to see his other woman. But I agreed to have the children because I wanted to see how they were and comfort them. I haven't seen them for a few days, not since he brought them here. I expect the next time I do, it will be at the funeral... When they release my sister's body."

Yvonne rose from her seat and took a card out of her bag. "Can I give you this?" she asked. "It's my number. You can call me anytime, if there is anything else you think we should know or if you have concerns. Once again, I am so sorry for your loss."

YVONNE KNOCKED on Jonathan Tudor's door and waited.

He widened a gap in his blinds to see who it was.

The DI gave him a wave.

"Do you have to?" he asked on opening the door.

"Is it inconvenient?" She raised a brow.

"Well, I... No, I suppose it's okay."

Yvonne flicked a glance around as he led her into the hall. "Where are David and Emily?"

He ran a hand through his hair. He looked crumpled and unkempt. "They're in school."

"Already?"

"We thought it best they have some structure to take their mind off things, and it gives me a chance to get on and deal with the things I need to. I have a funeral to arrange and Charlene's things to sort through."

"How are you financially?"

"We're okay. My employer is paying me a full salary for two weeks' compassionate leave, and we had some savings I can use for the funeral and the wake."

"Was there an insurance policy?" She inclined her head.

"Sadly not," he said, shaking his head. "We didn't think we needed them at our age. He sighed. We got that wrong."

"How are you coping?"

"Take a seat." He pointed to a small leather sofa where she and Dewi had sat on their last visit. "I have good days and bad days, I guess." He sat in an armchair at right angles to her. "I feel a bit lost, if I'm honest." He sighed. "I'm not sleeping well. It's the shock of it all, you see? I mean... You take people for granted, don't you? And then, one day, they are not there anymore. I've tried explaining it to the children. They know mummy's gone, but they struggle with why, and I don't blame them. I am also struggling with why."

"That is understandable." The DI cleared her throat. "Were you and Charlene happy?"

He frowned. "Why do you ask that?"

"Sometimes those who have lost someone feel guilt over a last conversation with them. Or some choice last words they wish they could take back. I was going to suggest that perhaps you shouldn't beat yourself up, if that were the case."

"We got on fine. Charlene was happy. We were good together."

"What about you?"

"What about me?"

"You said your wife was happy, but you failed to mention whether you were happy."

He looked towards the window. "I'm tired... I'm just exhausted. And lost."

"Have you considered bereavement counselling?"

He pointed to a bunch of leaflets on the coffee table. "Victim support gave me those. Bumf regarding all the services I can access. I pick them up to read them, and the words swim in front of me. They swirl around without sinking in. At the moment, I'm suffering from information overwhelm. I can't take any of it in. I lost my wife. Nothing makes sense anymore. I had the world all pegged out. I knew where everything was. It was all in its place, and now it isn't." He looked directly at her. "Can you understand that?"

She nodded. "Yes, of course..."

"People say things to me, and it goes in one ear and out the other."

"What about your children?"

"What about them?"

"How are they coping?"

"They're doing better than I expected, actually. They cry most at night. Charlene would always tuck them in. But... sometimes they forget she is gone and play like they always did. Until the next time it hits them."

"Perhaps the children could go to their aunt's house for a while until you feel less overwhelmed?"

"Do you mean Charmaine?" He frowned.

"Yes, to Charlene's sister."

"They have been there once since losing their mother, but I don't want them going to see her too often."

"Why not?"

"Charmaine can be abrasive."

"To the children? Or to you?"

"Look, does it matter?" He ran his hands through his hair. "Why are you here? Do you have news for me? Do you know the person responsible for my wife's death?"

"Not yet, but we are hard at work finding the answers to those very questions."

"Look, if you have nothing more to tell me, then I think you should go." He rose from his seat.

"You work for Kemikal?" The DI stayed where she was.

"Yes, why do you ask?"

"I understand your firm fulfils chemical orders for schools and laboratories in the area?"

"We do that work, yes." He frowned. "Wait, you don't think I did this? Do you? You think I stole chemicals from my place of employment and used them to harm other people and bump off my wife?"

"I didn't say any of that."

"You didn't need to... And I didn't. You've been speaking to Charmaine."

"Why do you think that?"

"She's convinced I'm having an affair. She said as much when I took the children over to see her after Charlene died. It's the reason I didn't take the children back there. I don't want her poisoning their minds against me."

"Why would she suspect something like that?"

"Because when something happens to the wife, it's the easiest option... pointing the finger at the husband."

"So, you're not having an affair?"

"No, I am not. Look, I had been working a lot of overtime, but that was so we could have holidays, and pay extra on the mortgage so we could eventually finish it early. You can't earn more without working more. I know Charlene found that difficult. Maybe she, too, thought I was having an affair. She should have asked me. I thought she was more distant recently, and I suspected I had upset her. I kept asking if I had done something wrong, and she would change the subject and act evasive. Perhaps she thought I was seeing someone else. But I wasn't. And I miss her. I miss us, together, with our children." His shoulders had rounded, and he looked like a man defeated.

Yvonne felt for him at that moment. Perhaps he hadn't been having an affair after all. "I really am sorry this happened to you and your family." The DI's eyes were soft with empathy. "I'll see myself out."

6

CLIMACTIC LEAD

Callum pushed a pen behind his ear as he approached Yvonne, who was perusing the information they had gathered on the attack in the park. "Climactic..." he said, notepad in hand.

"What's climactic?" she asked, her brow furrowed.

He grinned. "It's an environmental group; recently formed. They set themselves up as a rival to 'Just Stop Oil', who they object to because they think skeleton heads on the backs of the high-vis jackets are scary to children."

The DI grimaced. "Well, in that, I think they have a point."

"Climactic have been growing in scale and influence, and have a sizeable presence in Powys."

"Do you think they had something to do with what happened in the park?"

"There are criminal elements within the group. Some of the younger members have shoplifted for headlines, and seem to support activism only to enable their delinquent activities. They take advantage of the chaos they create."

"I see..."

"They take offence at the least little thing, and think anyone older than thirty has no clue how to run the world properly."

Yvonne rubbed her chin. "Have we any evidence they were at the park that day?"

Callum read from his notes. "They were handing leaflets to anyone who entered through the park's main gates."

The DI frowned. "Do we have any of these leaflets?"

"I don't think so..." Callum inclined his head. "Do you want me to get hold of some?"

"If anyone has a leaflet which was handed to them on that day, I would like you to bag it for testing. Speak to Dewi regarding instruction to forensics. And wear gloves."

"Do you think something was on the leaflets?"

"I don't know. But it is possible. If there was, it is likely to be harmless on its own, but I don't want you taking any chances until we know exactly what went on here. Also, see if either you or Dai can speak to someone in the NCA? See if they have any more information to help us know who, or what, we are looking for."

"Will do, ma'am."

AT FIVE-FOOT-TEN, thirty-five-year-old Kamal Bronson was a similar height to Dewi, as he greeted the DS and Yvonne at the door to his offices in Builth Wells. Athletically built, his muscles strained the fabric of his cotton shirt. They followed him along the corridor to the main office in a building made almost entirely from glass.

They passed what appeared to be a large gym on their left.

"Work hard; play hard," he said, on seeing the DI taking an interest.

"I'm here on my own until eleven," he explained. "My team is out on a reconnaissance mission, and my secretary is at a dental appointment."

Although the building was of modern steel and glass construction, conical roofs imbued a nod to older styles.

Yvonne's eyes fixated on stunning views over the hills. The Royal Welsh Show ground, where the famous agricultural festival occurred each summer, was visible in the distance. She cleared her throat. "This must be a lovely place to work?"

"It is..." He nodded. "These offices are only two years old. It's a privilege to see those views each day, though I must confess I sometimes forget to look."

"Are you from Wales, Mr Bronson?" she asked, as he pointed to a corner sofa for them to sit.

"My father grew up in Wales. His family was originally from America. My grandparents moved to Wales a couple of months before my father was born. My mother is from Pakistan. It took a while for her to adjust to the climate, but she ended up loving Wales every bit as much as my father. My parents now live in the Cardiff Bay Area." He sat on the corner suite, stretching his legs out in front of him. "So, to what do I owe this pleasure?" His perfectly manicured nails caught the DI's attention.

Yvonne took out her notebook. "We understand you have been buying up land in the Powys area to develop it?"

His brow furrowed. "Yes..."

"And you recently offered to buy part of Dolerw Park in Newtown?"

"I did, but they refused me. Shame..." He folded his

arms. "I could just imagine it with a riverside restaurant and cinema complex."

The DI scratched her cheek. "As I understand it, they already planned a riverside restaurant in the park, and the council approved the relevant planning permission some time ago."

"Yes, but mine would have been an improvement... More comprehensive. A proper day out for all the families who came to it."

"Were you disappointed?"

"When they turned down my proposal? Well, yes... Of course I was. I had spent years drawing up the plans, and really thought they would go for them. I would have developed a unique part of the river from the one already proposed, providing they allowed sufficient area for parking. Is that why you wanted to speak to me? To find out how disappointed I am?" Bronson raised both eyebrows. "Well, there you have your answer. I was totally dismayed."

"There was an incident in the park during the Eisteddfod. Several people fell ill. Two of them have since died." The DI scoured his face.

"Ah yes, I heard about that." He pursed his lips. "Were any of them from the town council?"

Yvonne frowned.

He held up his hands. "Hey, you don't think I'm serious? Do you think I would have hurt people so I could feel better about having my proposals turned down? What kind of man do you think I am?"

"People can be ruthless in business, Mr Bronson," Dewi said.

Kamal turned his attention to the DS. "Can they really? Wow, I didn't know that." His words oozed sarcasm.

Dewi's gaze remained firm. "We have yet to find a motive for the attack, and are investigating all avenues."

"Am I one of these avenues?" Kamal leaned forward. "I worked my ass off on that proposal. I don't offer my money lightly. But I'm hardly likely to ruin my business and personal reputation by poisoning a crowd attending the Welsh Eisteddfod. Even if I *was* ruthless enough."

"Where were you that day?" Yvonne asked.

"Do you mean if I wasn't in Dolerw Park making people sick?" He laughed.

"If you want to put it that way," she said, her face a mask, though his words had irked her. He evidently found it funny.

"I was giving a keynote speech at a business dinner arranged by clients. I have a burgeoning YouTube channel, and my followers expect me to attend events in person occasionally. And I do so willingly because it keeps my audience engaged and helps my business grow. We have one of the fastest growing portfolios on the planet right now." He grinned. "It feels like everybody wants a piece of me."

"Where was the business meeting?"

"Manchester."

"I see... How many employees do you have?"

"Fifty-five, all told. We have ten offices worldwide, four of which are in the UK. Bronson Holdings expanded by around fifty percent last year."

Yvonne nodded, although she failed to grasp the significance. The size of his portfolio was not important to her. The impact of the attack in the park was. "Councillors inform us you verbally abused one of their staff members over the phone when they rejected your offer."

He frowned. "I might have been a little rude. I'd had very little sleep after getting back from the United States the night before. But I wasn't abusive. It is not my fault if the person on the other end of the line is a snowflake. I merely made my feelings plain. I felt one or two of the council representatives had led me up the garden path. They led me to believe they would look kindly on my proposal, while I indulged certain councillors in a rather expensive seven-course meal."

"Was that an attempt to bribe them? That is always ill-advised." Yvonne's eyes were on her notepad.

"I had a reservation at the restaurant, anyway. I merely asked if they wished to join me. They did."

"I see..."

"What happened in the park, exactly?" His eyes bored into hers.

"We don't know. We are still investigating, and patients are undergoing tests."

"You said two had died?"

"We haven't had the results of their autopsies, yet. Those and other tests are happening out of the area."

"Above your pay grade, are they?"

If he was looking for a rise, she was determined not to satisfy him. "Thankfully."

"Well, if that is all, I ought to be getting on." He moved forward on the couch as though about to stand.

"That will be all for now." The DI nodded. "But we may wish to talk to you again. Don't leave the country."

He splayed his hands. "Feel free... You know where I am. But I cannot promise not to go on business trips."

7

POISONOUS INFORMATION

A break in the clouds rewarded Yvonne and Tasha with a welcome eruption of sunshine which spilled over the buildings and trees as they entered the wrought-iron gates of Dolerw Park. A day that started dull was fast improving as the DI led her partner through the car park and over the river bridge into the park-land proper, where people had fallen sick that fateful day.

Yvonne shared the gist of the story with the psychologist, then took her to see the still-cordoned areas where people had fallen ill, specifically pointing out the beer tent area where they believed the second exposure occurred. "The trouble is, Tasha, we don't know whether we are looking at a spree killer, a solitary psychopath harming for the hell of it, a revenge killer, or a group hell-bent on terrorising the community. Whatever the case, this attack was well-planned. The perp or perps had really thought this through."

Tasha nodded. "It's risky, too... From what you are telling me, if the perps had exposed themselves to both agents, they too would have ~~gotten~~ become sick and possibly died. They went to a lot of trouble to ensure that didn't happen. You think they left the second reagent at the beer tent? So, where was the first reagent?" The psychologist's brow furrowed in thought as she looked along the field at the various cordoned areas.

"That's what we have yet to find out. We tested park benches, and they proved negative. Several restaurants and the cinema were also negative. Car door handles in the car park yielded nothing. But I've requested tests on leaflets that were handed out by representatives of the environmental group 'Climactic' on that day. Their people were at the gates to the park, giving out brochures as crowds entered. I'm expecting the test results back tonight or early tomorrow."

Tasha ambled along, hands pushed into the pockets of her linen trousers. "I'm still getting my head around the nerve agent being used in the town. I mean, it was shocking when we heard Russians used it in Salisbury. But here? In our little Newtown? Why attack such a small place?"

Yvonne nodded. "I know what you are saying, but don't forget, on that day, little old Newtown was the representative of Wales. Some of Wales's finest and best talent was here, and a lot of visitors to the town. The Eisteddfod is a big event."

"You are right, of course." Tasha paused, rubbing her chin. "I hadn't thought of it that way. So, either this was an attack on the country by an individual or organisation, or they set it up to appear that way."

Yvonne scanned the line of hills above the town. "Do you think someone might have used the attack on the Eisteddfod to get rid of a spouse? Could they have thought the event a perfect cover?"

"Wow..." Tasha scratched her head. "That's a Machiavellian plot if ever I heard one. I guess, if someone had the means and the knowledge, they might in theory go to those lengths. But, honestly? I don't think it is likely. A person might go to a lot of trouble to cover up a murder that already happened, but to plan an attack like this to get rid of their partner? I don't see it. It's too complex. Spousal murder is usually far more pedestrian, I'm afraid. As horrible as such things are, they rarely involve this level of planning and risk to the perpetrator and the community at large. You sound like you have a suspect in mind?"

The DI pursed her lips. "One victim who died was a married mum of two. Rumours suggested her husband was having an affair. Crucially, he works for a chemical company about an hour away."

"I see..." Tasha looked at her partner. "Means, motive, and knowledge. I can see why you would look at him. But I stick to my original assessment. I think this was unlikely to have been a plot to get rid of a spouse. From what you have told me, it would have been a lottery regarding who would eventually become sick and die. They had to be exposed to reagents left in different locations. I think that is too hit-and-miss, as a method to target an individual. Keep an open mind and, by all means, investigate your suspect, but don't stop digging for others."

"We have others, actually." Yvonne outlined the circumstances of other suspicious characters in the case.

"There is so much to parse here. Can I have a day or two to think about it?" Tasha cocked her head, brow furrowed.

"Take as much time as you need." The DI smiled. "I know I am being cheeky asking for your opinion on your day off."

"Not at all. I think your case is fascinating, and I will enjoy pondering it. I shall give you my thoughts when I have pondered it through."

YVONNE AND DEWI were deep in conversation when Callum approached, somewhat out of breath. "What is it, Callum?" the DI asked, on seeing his wide, excited eyes. "You look like you've won the lottery?"

"Not quite, but it looks like you were on to something."

"Go on..."

"The leaflets from Climactic went to the labs at Porton Down for testing and proved positive for a constituent of the toxic nerve agent. We had confirmation a few minutes ago from the NCA. They are asking us to provide details of the chain of custody of the leaflets, from when the environmental group printed them until now. They also want all other leaflets destroyed. Uniform will take care of that with the help of a specialist cleanup agency. They are providing us with a specialist team, so they can do testing locally. We'll get our results faster in the future."

Dewi raised a brow. "Wow, Yvonne... The leaflets? That was brilliant thinking."

She shrugged. "I felt it was an obvious way of exposing many people to a reagent. And we knew only the adults became sick. We put that down to the second agent being at the beer tent, and that could still be the case, but people hand leaflets to adults because children would either not take them, would drop them, or sticky them up with something. People handing out leaflets thrust them in front of people. Have you noticed that? And our automatic response is to take things that are given to us in that way, even when we don't really want them."

"See? That is why you are a DI and I am a DS." Dewi grinned.

Yvonne gave him a push on the arm. "Go on with you..."

Laughing, she continued, "Anyway, you were the one with the nerve agent brainwave."

"I'm guessing you'll want to interview Anne Edwards or Damien Lloyd?" Callum cocked his head?

"The leaders of Climactic?"

"Yes, they are the co-founders."

"We'll want to interview both, but we can't divulge to them what we have found on the leaflets. We'll tell them we are interviewing everyone who was there that day, and we'll get onto the leaflets and who handled them as we go."

"Right you are, ma'am."

8

ACTIVE ACTIVISTS

Anne Edwards and Damien Lloyd, the leaders of the environmental activist group, Climactic, had agreed to come in to the station for interview.

The DI explained she would question them separately when they tried to insist on a joint interview during the phone call. She knew they would confer beforehand, but with skilful questioning, she hoped to expose any attempt to hide or manipulate the truth.

Both had turned down the offer of having a solicitor present, saying they didn't feel they needed one, and that it would be a waste of the charity's funds.

Twenty-four-year-old Anne was the first to be interviewed.

Dewi showed her into the interview room where the DI waited, reading her notes. The DS took his seat next to Yvonne.

She was tall, at around five-foot-ten, with a firm chin, and piercing green eyes. Her hair, in a reddish-brown bob, had two coloured slides on each side holding back the hair from her face. A green streak ran down one side. Though clearly slim, she wore an oversized yellow tee shirt, and had her hands pushed into the pockets of equally large dungarees. A pair of red bother-boots completed the ensemble. She slumped herself down in the chair opposite the detectives.

"There is a mug of tea for you, if you would like one? Milk and sugar too, if you want it?" Dewi pushed the mug towards her.

"Is the milk vegan?" She asked, eyeing the hot beverage.

The DS grimaced. "Er, I don't think so. I believe it's cow's milk."

Anne pushed the mug away from her, as though it was disease ridden.

Yvonne cleared her throat. "Ms Edwards-"

"It's Anne," the woman interjected. "I'm not posh. I'll feel weird if you refer to me as Ms all the way through this."

"Very well, Anne, thank you for coming in to see us today. I will ask you again if you wish to have a solicitor present for this interview."

She shook her head.

"You could face serious charges..."

Anne frowned. "For what? I have done nothing wrong, and I am not scared. And, as we told you, we don't wish to waste our supporters' money on legal teams or anything else unless absolutely necessary. And since I have done nothing I am ashamed of, I don't feel the need for legal counsel."

"Then can you begin by telling us a little about your organisation, and your connection with it?"

The woman shrugged, hands still in her dungarees pockets. "Sure... We're an environmental charity called 'Climactic'. So-called, because we are dedicated to saving the climate and take positive action to do so."

"And what is your position within the group?"

"I am the joint CEO, along with Damien."

"And how big is the charity?"

"At last count, we had over twelve thousand members, and growing."

"You may already know that several people fell ill, and some sadly passed away, during the Eisteddfod in Newtown. We are interviewing everybody who was there that day to gain an understanding of what happened and why."

Anne frowned. "So, you want to know if we saw anything?"

"Did you?"

"The first I knew there was a problem was when I saw crowds of people leaving at the same time. I heard someone shouting there was danger, but I couldn't see where the issue was. I remember moving out into the car park, as there was a panic on to get out of Dolerw. My instinct was to go with the rush of people heading out until I could find out what was happening."

"Where were you when the first shouts went up? When did you realise was something wrong?"

"I was on the bridge, looking over the water. I was on my way to the field, after talking to our guy who was at the main gates."

"The representative handing out leaflets?"

"Yes... Gary Jones. He's a local who offered to help last minute. The girl who was to help us that day couldn't be there."

"Was that your main reason for being at the event? To hand out leaflets?"

"That, and to man our stall in the park. The table had our leaflets and a few environmentally friendly craft goods made by charity members. In the end, it was Gary who was at the stall for most of the time."

"Would Damien have been at the stall at any point?"

"Yes, she nodded. Our stall was close to the park gates. I think he popped back to it occasionally."

"I see..." Yvonne took out a copy one of Climactic's leaflets, and pushed it towards Edwards, her eyes not leaving the woman's face. "Is this one of leaflets you were handing out that day?"

Anne ran her eyes over the cover. "Looks like it, yes."

"Pick it up, have a good look. You need to be sure."

Edwards flicked her eyes to the DI's own. "I am sure. I can see it is one of ours."

Yvonne scribbled on her notepad. "Where did the leaflets come from?"

"We had them printed at our office, I think?"

"You think? You're the joint CEO. Surely you would know where you had them printed?"

Anne pressed her lips hard together before replying. "We made them in Wrexham, at our head office. I believe Damien reeled them off and boxed them up."

"And how did they get to Newtown?"

"We brought them with us in the van."

"Were they ever in the custody of anyone else other than yourself, Damien, or Gary?"

"Not as far as I know..." Edwards frowned. "What is this, anyway? What is so special about our leaflets? Why would it matter who had them, and when?"

"Were they left alone at the stall at any point?"

"They may have been, yes. Gary manned the stall most of the time, but I think I left the stall unmanned while I took over for a bit... I needed the loo. No-one was likely to steal stacks of our leaflets. I thought them pretty safe. And someone had already snapped up the few homemade goods we had."

"Did the leaflets appear to be wet at any point? As in soaked or splashed?"

"No... It was a dry day, and I didn't notice them getting wet. But, as I stated, Gary spent the most time with them. I should speak to him if I were you." Anne frowned. "You are asking strange questions."

"It's my job, Anne. And I fully intend questioning Gary, too. Aside from when they were with yourself or Gary, was Damien a custodian of the leaflets at all? I mean, after he printed them?"

"Yes. I think he took them home after they came off the printer. We were setting off early the following morning, so he loaded the van the night before."

"Thank you, Anne."

"Is that it? Can I go now?" She asked, looking bemused and irritated.

"You can, but we may wish to speak with you again."

"Fine." Anne's eyes flashed fire. "It's not a crime to care about the environment."

Yvonne's gaze remained steady. "I know."

DAMIEN WAS TALLER than his female counterpart, but only marginally, at five-foot-eleven. He was also as lean as his vegan colleague. But that is where the similarities ended. Though Anne had dressed in baggy clothing to hide her slight build, Lloyd appeared to revel in it, choosing figure-hugging jeans and shirt that emphasised his well-developed musculature. There was a hint of danger about him, though the DI couldn't quite put her finger on why.

His hair was dark and wavy, and he had hawkish brown eyes and sallow skin — as though he had spent years courting the sun. At twenty-nine, he had a lithe confidence about him, and seemed not in the least phased at being called for a police interview. Like Anne, he had refused legal counsel, stating he had no need of it.

"Would you prefer Damien? Or Mr Lloyd?" the DI asked.

He shrugged. "Damien is fine."

"Very well, Damien. Thank you for attending today."

"Will this take long? Only, I have to be back in Wrexham by five this afternoon."

Yvonne checked her watch. "It's only two o'clock. You should be back in plenty of time, even if you allow two hours for the travel."

"Fine." He leaned back in the chair, legs stretched out under the table; crossed at the ankles.

"What time did you arrive in Newtown on the morning of the Eisteddfod?"

His brow furrowed as he thought about it. "Er, early. A little after seven, I think? We had set up our stall and laid everything out by about half-past nine that morning."

"Were you looking forward to it?"

"Sure. I thought we might sign a few people up as supporters of our charity."

"And did you?"

"We signed up nineteen, I think?"

"Who is the custodian of your charity's funds?"

"Technically, both Anne and myself. But she leaves most of the running to me."

"Is there an official oversight?"

He narrowed his eyes. "Why? Do you worry I might be on the take? The environmental issues we face are far too serious for that." His voice deepened and grated with irritation.

"I merely asked, Damien."

"And I merely answered... Next?"

The DI didn't react. "I understand you were hopeful about getting interest through leaflet distribution?"

"I took some to hand out, yeah."

"You printed off a thousand?"

"About that many."

"Did you give them all out?"

He shook his head. "We distributed around three hundred of them, which wasn't bad, actually. But we've done better at some events, and worse at others."

"And you printed them off the night before?"

"Yes." He frowned. "Why so interested in my leaflets?"

The DI drew forth the leaflet copy again. "Does this look like one of yours?"

He twisted his head to peer at it. "Yes, it looks like one of ours."

"You can pick it up and examine it if you want to be sure."

"I can see it fine. It appears to be one of our leaflets."

"There is a recall of these leaflets. Did you know about it?"

"I had a letter through the door from the police, asking to have the rest the other day. I wondered why they would want them, but I assumed it was to make sure we were not saying anything too dangerous in our message. You know, like anything that conflicts with the official narrative."

Yvonne exchanged glances with Dewi. "Have you handed them in, Damien?"

"I gave them in yesterday. Will I be getting them back?"

She shook her head. "I'm afraid not."

"Am I going to be paid for them? Even though I printed them myself, it still cost us in time, paper, and ink. None of those things comes cheap."

"You can apply to be compensated."

"What did you want them for, anyway?"

"We think they may have contributed to making people sick."

He swallowed. "What?"

"We think the leaflets may have been a factor in people becoming ill."

"My leaflets? How?" His mouth hung open.

"We found contamination on them."

"That is ridiculous. I don't understand. What were they contaminated with?"

"Were they left alone at any point?"

"Not until they were in our stall at the festival." He frowned. "We often leave the table unattended for a bit. How would that lead to contamination? Did someone spill something on them?"

"You tell me..." Yvonne inclined her head. "Did they look wet at any point?"

"Not that I noticed."

"Were any handed back for that reason, or for any reason?"

"Not that I recall. No-one gave any back to me. I saw a few in the bin later, mind."

"Did you feel ill at any point that day? Or the night before?"

"No, I felt fine. And I still feel fine."

"What about your helper, Gary?"

"I haven't seen him since, but he was fine when we left him at around five that afternoon. We were all talking about the panic that was on that day, and the fact people fell ill. All three of us were okay."

"Did any of you consume beer from the beer tent on the grounds?"

He shook his head. "No, we didn't. I had a couple of cans when I got back to Wrexham. As far as I know, Anne and Gary consumed the cola and juice they brought with them. Drinks at venues feel overpriced, and we aim to look after our supporters' money. Back to your earlier question... Personally, I did not leave the leaflets unattended. Gary Jones might have, as we gave no specific instruction to him not to. It might be worth asking Gary."

"We will, thank you."

"So, how did our leaflets make people sick? What was the contamination?" He was frowning again.

"We are investigating the exact nature of the contamination."

He folded his arms. "It must have happened when we weren't looking. I didn't notice any being damp or dirty, but it was a hot day... Maybe they were wet and then dried? That is the only thing I can think of. But I don't know what might have been in that park that would have made people sick, unless it was off meat, or something?" He searched their eyes, still fishing for details, and what the contaminant might have been.

The DI wondered if he was playing at innocence. He was hard to read.

"WHAT DO YOU THINK?" she asked Dewi as they walked back, following the interview.

"I don't know. He rubbed his chin. I wouldn't put it past

him to do something criminal, but he seemed genuinely surprised about the leaflets. He will probably quiz Anne and Gary about them, even though we have asked him not to."

"But did you notice that neither he nor Anne touched the leaflets when I asked them to pick them up and look at them? Damien could have contaminated the leaflets, but did he have the means and motive?" The DI scratched her head. "If they left the leaflets alone above once, our suspect could still be anyone. How are we doing for CCTV in the surrounding area?"

"We have it, and officers have been going through hours and hours of footage."

"Have them looked specifically at that stall. If someone contaminated the leaflets while Climactic left the stall unmanned, we may have it on camera. And, if we don't have official footage, cast the net wider and ask the public for any photographs or video taken at the Eisteddfod. Someone may have caught it unwittingly."

"Will do, ma'am."

9

THE WOODEN CHAIRS

"Ma'am..." Dai approached them. "Someone smeared the second constituent of the nerve agent onto the backs and seats of the wooden chairs outside of the beer tent."

"We have that confirmed?"

"Yes, people may have become exposed from sitting or leaning on them, and touching them with their hands. That makes sense, because it is where people began feeling ill. And, if you think about it, beer glasses can be damp with condensation. That may have helped the reaction between the reagents."

"Of course... Well done, Dai. Where are the chairs now?"

"Researchers have them at Porton Down, and they will destroy them once testing is complete."

"Have they said what the final nerve agent was?"

"No, they haven't, Yvonne. They are playing their cards close to their chest at the moment."

"Have they or the NCA said how much we can divulge about the incident? We've still got the nation's press hanging on our doorstep."

Dai shrugged. "Best speak with the DCI, ma'am. If anyone knows, it will be him."

"I'll do that. In the meantime, speak to Dewi about CCTV footage and the Climactic Environmentalist group's stall."

"Got it."

~

"Ah, Yvonne... Come in. I'm glad you came to see me. I wanted to ask you about the Eisteddfod poisonings, and how the case is progressing. There's a lot of pressure coming from above on this. I know we are not the only service involved in the investigation, but the powers that be want answers."

"I know, sir. We are making progress, and have confirmed the locations where the perpetrator placed each of the two chemical reagents. The mixing of these substances created the toxin that made people sick. We believe the poisonings were meticulously planned, but we cannot determine yet if the perpetrator targeted specific individuals."

"I see..." He nodded. "Were both of the substances left in the park?"

"Yes, sir."

"Christ!" He ran a hand through his hair. "Not what you expect to happen in rural Wales."

"It is possible they targeted it at the Eisteddfod. That would be the likely conclusion to draw." She frowned.

"You look doubtful, Yvonne?"

"I am unsure whether criminals targeted the Eisteddfod, or used the festival as a cover to kill someone specific. That is what I am trying to get my head around, sir. The team has identified several suspects, all of whom had potential motive and the capability to carry out this attack."

"Well, that's great... So there could be a breakthrough soon?"

"We are interviewing them all. I will keep you informed of progress."

"Good..." He sighed. "I don't need to remind you of the urgency. With two people dead already, we don't want another incident before we get the perpetrator behind bars."

"I know, sir. I was going to ask you how much we can say to the press?"

"As little as we can get away with until we have a suspect or suspects in custody."

"Reporters are everywhere, and they are becoming more insistent."

"I understand, but we balance that against the fear the public will feel if they know there are killers with nerve agent loose in the community. When you make an arrest, we will inform the public about the true nature of the incident."

"Shouldn't we at least warn people to keep washing their hands?"

"Sure, you can do that. But for the moment, do so as though it is in relation to communicable diseases... Perhaps a new COVID variant?"

"Right..." The DI pursed her lips.

The DCI's mind was already turning to other things. "All right, well, good luck out there. Let me know if you need my help."

"Thank you, I will."

10

LIES, MORE LIES, AND PHOTOGRAPHS

Twenty-one-year-old Gary Jones looked about eighteen. He was red-faced and sweaty, as the DI led him into the interview room, and cleared his throat several times, wiping wet hands on the front of his jeans. His wiry blonde hair appeared windswept and resistant to his damp-handed attempts to tame it.

Yvonne did her best to put him at ease with a smile; pouring him water from a jug on the table. "Thank you for coming in, Gary."

He gave her a nod, plonking himself awkwardly in the seat opposite. The plastic bag he was carrying slipped to the floor. He picked it up again. "It's just my books," he said, referring to the two paperbacks spilling out of the carrier. "They checked them at the front desk, and let me bring them in."

The DI grinned. "It's okay... I didn't think you had a bomb in there. If I'd thought that, I would probably be under the desk by now."

He smiled at that, and his shoulders relaxed.

"I understand you were helping the environmental group, Climactic, at the Eisteddfod?"

He nodded. "I looked after their stall for a few hours while they went around the park talking to people."

"You were handing out leaflets at the show. Am I right?"

"Yes, I gave them out on behalf of Climactic. Some people took them from the table themselves, but mostly I gave them to people as they passed through the gates. Our stall was right by the entrance."

"Clever strategy..." The DI pursed her lips. "Did you leave the leaflets alone at any point? For example, when going to the toilet block?"

"I did, yes. I visited the toilets at least twice during the time I was there." His brow furrowed.

"What is it?" Yvonne inclined her head.

"There was a woman carrying a tray. I think it had food on, and she was taking it to one of the other stalls. She tripped over, and I ran to help her. That was the only other time I left the stall. There was that incident, and a couple of trips to the toilet. I honestly didn't think anyone would steal leaflets, so I thought it would be okay to leave them for a few minutes."

The DI held up a hand. "Oh, yes... absolutely. Gosh, you can't go all day without going to the loo. You did nothing wrong there."

He cleared his throat again. "Why did you ask me in?" He blushed.

"We are interviewing everyone who was at the park that day to establish what happened, and why people fell sick. The stall holders would have had a good view of people coming and going, but we would like to know from you what you saw that day. Did you notice anything that made you concerned or suspicious?"

He shook his head. "The most exciting thing that happened to me at the Eisteddfod was the lady falling over, and me going to help." His eyes widened. He looked horrified, holding both hands up. "Oh God, I didn't mean... It wasn't exciting. I don't find people falling over the highlight of my day."

Yvonne laughed despite herself. "It's okay, Gary. I knew what you meant. Don't panic... You're fine."

"I thought she had hurt herself," he continued. "Her knee hit the curb where the road in meets the grass. I was worried, in case she needed medical attention. But, when I got there, she was just sore and embarrassed, and needed help to get the packs of sandwiches back onto her tray."

"Could you describe the woman for me?" The DI held her pen at the ready.

"Yes, er... She was young. About my age, I would say. Long dark hair, and slim. She was wearing a red dress with tiny white flowers on it. I can't remember what she had on her feet, I'm afraid. But I remember, when she thanked me, thinking what a nice voice she had. I don't know her name. She didn't tell me. But her accent was posh."

"So she was well-spoken?"

"Yes."

"And how long would you say you helped her for?"

"Not longer than a few minutes, I would say."

"Did you see where she went after that? Where was she taking the tray?"

He shook his head. "I don't know... She disappeared into the crowd, and that was that."

"I see... When you got back to your stall, had anything changed about it?"

He frowned. "In what way?"

"Did the stacks of leaflets look like they had when you left them to help the woman?"

He shrugged. "I think so?"

"Did you handle the leaflets right away? To give them to new arrivals?"

"Yes, I did."

"Did any feel damp to you?"

"The leaflets? Or the new arrivals?"

The DI grinned. "The leaflets."

"Not that I recall. Should they have done? I don't remember it raining that day."

"I'm simply curious. There was a sprinkler in the location, apparently. It obviously wasn't that close to you."

"Oh... No, it wasn't."

She felt guilty, telling a white lie to explain herself, but the current secrecy around the case gave her little choice. "Do you support Climactic, Gary? Are you an environmentalist?"

He cocked his head while he thought about it. "I care about the environment, yes. I don't support all the tactics employed by the group, though."

"Such as?"

"Well, I don't think we should disrupt traffic, or paint slogans on banks, I guess? It feels... criminal to me."

"Very noble." The DI nodded. "Considering others is a good thing to do."

"Thank you, I thought so."

"And what do you think of Anne and Damien?"

"They seem dedicated to the cause. They believe in what they are doing."

"What about the group's tactics?"

He shrugged. "They seem prepared to do what they have to get the job done and achieve their goals."

"Do you agree with the things they do?"

"I haven't seen them do anything too bad. But they don't come to this area that often, and I don't go to national rallies. I do little bits to help support the group, but many are from a distance. I give money occasionally, and sign petitions... that sort of thing."

"I see... Is there anything else you would like to tell me about Climactic, or the Eisteddfod?"

Gary shook his head.

"Very well then, Mr Jones. You are free to go. Here is my card for if you remember anything else."

"Thank you," he said, placing the card in the back pocket of his jeans.

∿

"Ma'am..." Callum approached the DI as she returned to CID.

"What is it?" She checked her watch, her stomach rumbling. It was lunchtime.

"It's Charmaine Davies, Charlene's sister. She wants to see you; says it is urgent."

"Did she say what it was about?" Yvonne's brow furrowed.

"She insisted she see you." The DC grimaced. "Wouldn't take no for an answer, and is waiting in reception."

"Very well." Yvonne sighed. "Could you do me a favour? Could you nip out at some point and pick me up a tuna and cucumber sandwich? I'm starving."

"Sure, no problem." He nodded. "Want a drink with it?"

"An orange juice would be fab."

"I'll go in about ten mins." He grinned. "You might be a

little while longer." He flicked his head toward reception. "Good luck..."

"Thanks. I suspect I'll need it."

Charmaine sat in the waiting room, crossing and uncrossing her legs; repeatedly looking at her watch. She appeared to have been waiting for some time.

"Mrs Davies?" Yvonne called to her. "This way."

Charmaine grabbed her bag and coat and followed the DI to an interview room; taking a seat before pulling out her phone.

"Someone is in a hurry?" Yvonne narrowed her eyes. "What's going on?"

"I told you he was having an affair." Charmaine's eyes flashed angrily. "I was bloody-well right."

She pointed to the screen on her mobile. "See?"

Yvonne took a seat opposite, accepting the phone from Charlene's sister. "What is it am I looking at?"

"That is Jonathan Tudor, kissing some fancy woman in his vehicle. I took that from inside my car, when I saw them parked in the street outside of my sister's home!" She gritted her teeth. "I just knew it. It was a little after dark, and they probably thought no-one would see them. They didn't reckon with me being there, did they? I took out my mobile and shot those two photos."

"They're a little blurry..." The DI held the mobile further from her, as though it would help make the pictures clear, turning the phone slightly to appreciate the angle from which Charmaine had taken them.

"They are a bit, but that is because I had to snap them in a hurry before they saw me. His headlights were off, but mine were on and I could clearly see them. They didn't know it was me because they couldn't see beyond my lights. But I could see them, and I have banged them to rights."

"Who is the woman?" Yvonne asked.

"I don't know." Charmaine grimaced, her face riddled with disgust. "I've never seen her before. Some floozie obviously, and my sister not even in her grave... I can't believe the front of that man."

"And you are sure this is Jonathan?"

"Yes, of course... Can't you see?"

"I'm not sure this is clear enough to use as evidence of anything."

"Well, I could see him really well, and I know his vehicle. I should have taken a shot of his numberplate too, but I didn't think of that. It all happened so fast. I thought the quality of the photo would be better. Soon after I took that shot, they drove off. I think they must have had a babysitter, because I saw a different female leave when he got back later on."

"You were watching the house?"

"Of course. Wouldn't you have been, if it was your sister lying dead while her husband is having it away with someone else? I mean, the front of the man."

"I understand you are angry, Charmaine, but he isn't doing anything illegal."

"No, but it's a motive, isn't it? And he works at a chemical factory and all. You must look into it now, mustn't you? He had the means and motive to poison my sister. And all because of some floozie, he met somewhere."

"That is rather an enormous leap, Mrs Davies. You must be careful about saying things like that. It could be defamatory."

"I lost my sister," Charmaine spat.

"I understand, and I get you are angry, but you really must be careful throwing accusations of poisoning without evidence. May we take copies of the photographs?"

"Yes, it's why I brought them here. You can question him again. This time, with something to back it up."

"Thank you." Yvonne stood. "Are you happy to wait while I take this phone to the team for them to extract the pictures?"

"Yes." Charmaine leaned back, folding her arms.

"Very well. I shall return in a minute."

BACK IN CID, the DI handed Charmaine's phone to Callum. "Can you pull the last two photographs from the camera roll, please? She alleges them to be of Charlene Tudor's husband, kissing another woman. Ms Davies believes he is having an affair, and that he carried out the attack in the park in order to do away with his wife."

"Okay... They're a little distorted..."

"I know, but it is all she has, I'm afraid. And she has a point. He flat out denied having an affair to myself and Dewi. Was he simply hiding ungentlemanly behaviour, or is Charmaine right and there is more to it?"

"I'll get it done now. Is she waiting downstairs?"

"She is."

"Right-oh, I will copy them, and get the phone back to her. Unless you need to see her again?"

"Not today... I need food." Yvonne grinned. "Tread lightly. She is in a feisty mood down there."

Callum laughed. "Noted."

11

A CLANDESTINE AFFAIR

"I've been thinking about your case," Tasha said, as she handed Yvonne a glass of her favourite Chardonnay that evening.

For once, they ate outside in the garden under the cherry tree. The evening was warm and dry, perfect for alfresco dining, and they were looking forward to the liver and onions which had slow-cooked through the day.

"And what are your thoughts?" The DI asked, accepting the glass and taking the first sip. She ran her eyes over the distant hills. It really was a gorgeous evening. She brought her gaze back to her partner, now seated.

"Given the circumstances of the attack, the importance of the Eisteddfod to the people of Wales, and the size of the crowd, I am leaning towards this having been an attempt to shock the community or the country at large, or revenge for a perceived wrong."

"Go on..."

"My opinion is the perp is an individual, not an organisation. It looks like a terror attack at first glance, but that may be misleading. I don't believe a terror group did this. They would likely have chosen a bigger town, and a more memorable venue... No offence to Newtown. I think it more likely that this was a personal mission by an individual who lives or works close by... Probably within a fifty-mile radius. The perp will have cased the park and nearby streets prior to the attack, and I suspect they feel comfortable in the area. They knew where they could leave the contaminants and not get caught."

Yvonne nodded. "They smeared the second contaminant on chairs in the lower field, where there is no CCTV."

"Right... And the leaflets?"

"What about the leaflets?"

"Was there a CCTV camera near those?"

"There was..."

"Have you checked it?"

"The footage has been gone through, and we found no evidence of anyone spraying anything on them."

"Did someone impregnate or spray the paper beforehand?"

"They might have, but then we would suspect the environmentalist who printed them off."

"It would be a good place to start. Also, Yvonne, environmentalists can get away with spraying places without people thinking too much about it. They often daub paint, etc and people see the substance as harmless, even if the perpetrators are creating a nuisance. It might not stick in people's minds the way it would, seeing someone else do something like that."

"You have a point..."

"Hence, an activist would have greater confidence, perhaps, to carry out an attack like this."

Yvonne frowned. "Except I don't see environmentalists

wanting to physically harm people, or risk killing members of the community in order to achieve their aims? That doesn't sit right with me..."

"I agree so. If it was one of your activists, they did it for deeply personal reasons."

"Wow..." The DI leaned back in her seat. "Now that gives me pause for thought."

～

ALTHOUGH WARM, the day had been dogged by drizzle. The DI popped open her umbrella as she left the car, while Dewi lifted the collar on his coat to keep the rain off his neck.

They rang Jonathan Tudor's bell and waited.

The man who opened the door appeared fresh and better rested than the one who had let them in only eight days before. There were no creases in his shirt and jeans, and no hairs were out of place as he showed them through to the lounge.

The DI's gaze turned to the garden, through the window where she had last seen the children playing on the swings. All play equipment stood silent now; the garden was empty. "Where are Emily and David?" she asked, her eyes returning to their father.

"They are in school." He cleared his throat. "I thought it would be better for them to be with their friends, and to be thinking about other things; not moping about here. Everything in this house reminds them of their mother."

"I see..." Yvonne pressed her lips together. "How are they coping?"

"They are doing all right, considering. It isn't easy for any of us, but we are taking each day as it comes and things are getting easier. I think Charlene would be proud of us. Please, take a seat," he added, pointing to the sofa.

Yvonne and Dewi did as they were told, while Tudor sat in the armchair at right angles to them.

The DI sat back, her pensive gaze on Jonathan's face. "You appear to be on top of things, Mr Tudor. That is admirable. But how are you coping with the heartache, really? You look as though you are sleeping better now?"

He nodded. "It took a few days for me to get more than a couple of hours a night. But I am having quality sleep now and feeling better for it."

"Are you lonely?"

He shrugged, his cheeks colouring. "I feel it some days more than others. I miss Charlene padding about here. But the children keep me busy, and I cannot mope when they are around. I guess it is worse when they are in school. Times like now, I dread the emptiness and the silence."

"Are you back at work?"

"I will go back next week, part time until I have properly sorted childcare. My mother can have them some days, but Wednesdays and Fridays, I have no-one to pick them up from school."

"What about Charmaine?" Yvonne inclined her head. "Can she not pick them up? She fetches her own children, and I am sure she would give them tea before you collected them."

His face became a mask. "I'm not asking Charmaine."

"Why?"

"I already told you... She is not my favourite person right now. She outright accused me of having an affair. I don't want my children being poisoned by that."

"Are you?"

"Am I what?" He frowned.

"Having an affair?"

"I thought we had that conversation on your last visit here?"

"We did."

"Well, then..."

"Are you afraid of what people may think of you? Or something else?"

He narrowed his eyes. "I don't follow."

"Are you afraid to admit you are seeing someone because we will judge you?"

He swallowed. "Have you been to see her again? Did she convince you this time?"

"Who is she, Jonathan? And when did you meet her?"

"You have been speaking to my wife's sister, haven't you?"

"Someone saw you with another woman; in a clinch, in your car."

"Who saw us?"

"So, you are seeing another woman?"

He ran a hand through his hair. "It's not what it seems."

"So, tell us how it is? When did you meet? How did the affair begin?"

"We'd been friends for a year. They accused me of having an affair long before we began seeing each other."

"Which was when? Was Charlene still alive?"

His gaze was now on the empty garden. "It was before my wife died, yes." He put his head in his hands.

"How long before?"

"I don't know exactly. Maybe a couple of months?"

"Did Charlene know?"

"She suspected, but I didn't confirm it. I know this will sound selfish, but I didn't want to lose her."

"And you were afraid you would?"

"Yes."

"Did she tell you she was leaving?"

"She raised the subject, yes."

"Did she mention possible divorce?"

"She did."

"And how did that make you feel?"

"Terrified."

"Why?"

"Because I still loved her, and I love my kids."

"Did she threaten to take the children?"

"Yes."

"What did you say?"

"To what?"

"Did she ask you to give up the other woman?"

"No, she didn't."

"Would you have?"

He didn't answer.

"What did you say to her when she asked about divorce?"

"I told her I loved her and the children, and asked her not to leave."

"But you didn't offer to give up the other woman?"

"I was confused, and I didn't know what I wanted. I only knew that her threat to leave frightened me, even though I was questioning everything about my life at the time. Boredom had set into my marriage, and the affair was exciting. But when Charlene threatened to leave, things became non-boring really fast. Perhaps I was guilty of wanting my cake and eating it."

"What about the children?"

"What about them?"

"Did they know about the affair?"

The shake of his head was vigorous. "No... I couldn't tell them... not even now. They need time."

"Are you planning on continuing the relationship?"

"I tried to end it, but missed Debbie too much, and always ended up calling her. When my wife died. I ended it for good, or so I thought. But I've been feeling so lonely, and when Debs phoned to ask how I was, we started seeing each other again."

"So her name is Debbie... Did you meet at work?"

"No... We met in the supermarket, of all places. This one Saturday, I nipped out to do a spot of food shopping and I kept bumping into this female in the store. Not literally, but we keep meeting by accident in different aisles. In the end, I laughed and accused her of stalking me. We chuckled about it but, the following Saturday, I found myself there again; picking up a few bits. And there she was. This time, she accused me of stalking and we got chatting. That is how it all started. And, believe me, if I could go back and change all of that, I would. I was happily married, and I wasn't looking for anything. It hit me out of the blue. She said it was the same for her. We neither of us expected it to happen."

"Did Charlene give you an ultimatum?"

"No, like I said, she didn't think we could move on from it. Even if I had stopped seeing Debbie, my wife may never have forgiven me."

"But you tried giving up the affair to save your marriage?"

"I paused things for a few weeks. It didn't change Charlene's mind."

"Why did you lie to us before?"

"Because I felt, if you knew about the affair, you might think I killed my wife."

"Did you?"

"No." His brow furrowed.

"You had the potential means at your disposal?"

"What? Because I work for a chemical company?"

"Yes."

"Oh, for Christ's sake!" He ran his hands through his hair. "I can't help where I work. It doesn't make me a murderer."

"It doesn't, but you evidently felt you had the means and a motive, or you wouldn't have hidden it from us. What were you afraid of, really? If you are innocent, there is no proof to be found. And you are innocent until proven guilty."

"In a court of law, maybe... But, to people out there? If it were the court of public opinion, they would find me guilty as charged. Debbie and I would be all over the local and national rags and social media. They would struggle to find unbiased jurors."

"What makes you think we would inform the press of our suspicion?"

"Wouldn't you? At one of your press conferences? When the pressure was on, and they wanted a name, wouldn't you have fed me to them?"

"We don't work like that, Mr Tudor."

"The minute I went into the station for questioning, the papers and everyone else would have had me pegged for it."

"We wouldn't be giving the press your name unless we charged you. And we wouldn't charge you without evidence."

"I suppose you'll be speaking to my employers?"

"We may ask them to do an inventory, yes."

"In case I stole from them?"

"In case anyone did."

"Fine." He sighed. "Do what you have to. I have nothing to hide."

"Thank you."

"Will that be all?" he asked. "Only, I have to pick the children up in thirty minutes, and I was hoping to get tea cooking before I do."

"Yes, of course, we'll be going." Yvonne rose to her feet, followed by Dewi. "Thank you for your time."

12

SOLUTION VANISHING?

"Ma'am..." Dai was waiting for her when she returned.

"What is it?" She hung her wet coat on a radiator, standing the umbrella next to it.

"We found something on CCTV footage from the Eisteddfod. I think you should take a look. Maybe something; maybe nothing."

"Okay, hit me with it." She walked with him to his desk, where he had paused at an image of a figure in a hoodie who was mid-stride.

"This person had their hood up on what was a blistering day."

"So they were up to no good?"

"Highly likely, I would say. Now, watch this..." Dai pressed play on the image, and the figure approached the gates to the park, stood in front of the Climactic stall for four seconds, then moved away. "Did you see that?" Dai asked.

"Play it again." Yvonne leaned in.

"What did you see?" Dai paused the footage after they had viewed it again.

"From the back, it looked like he was taking something and putting it under his top?"

"Right... He was definitely doing something at that stall. I, too, felt he was stealing something, but I didn't know what that would be."

"Could he simply have been taking a leaflet?"

"I would agree he could, except for the way he did it. His body language screams up to no good. I mean, he checked left and right and was messing with the front of his hoodie. My gut tells me he was on edge."

"Can we get an identification?" The DI studied the figure on the screen. "Shame we can't see his face. Have you looked through the rest of the footage to see if we have a front image?"

"I have and, so far, no luck. A similar figure comes back again, about thirty minutes later. Again, we only see him from behind, and there were a lot more people in that area of the park, so we can only see part of him. May not be the same person, but I will do what I can to get it enhanced."

"Yes, keep on it. We need a way of identifying the person. If nothing else, it would be good to know his height and approximate weight. That would be a start at least."

"I'll see what I can do." Dai nodded. "Leave it with me."

Dewi rubbed his chin. "That hoodie, it is very like the one Damien Lloyd had tied around his waist when he came here to be interviewed."

"I agree. It was similar." Yvonne pursed her lips, her face determined. "We'll get him back in for questioning. Perhaps he tampered with those leaflets while they were on the stall."

KEMIKAL HAD their primary units at an industrial complex on the outskirts of Shrewsbury.

Yvonne and Dewi parked on the tarmac near the entrance of the one-storey building, and walked towards the double doors which opened automatically.

A forty-something male in a shirt and tie, sleeves rolled up, came towards them, holding out his hand. "DI Giles?" He directed this at Dewi.

The DS nodded towards Yvonne. "This is DI Giles; I am DS Hughes."

Yvonne smiled at them both. "And you must be Mr Burton?"

"Kevin Burton, but plain old Kevin will do."

"Thank you for agreeing to talk with us."

"No problem." He grinned. "It breaks up the day. Come through to the office. Would you like a coffee?"

They passed two other gentlemen who were signing documents and checking over consignments for delivery, as others loaded stacks of boxes onto a transit van.

"I'd love one, thanks." Dewi nodded.

"Milk; no sugar." The DI said, as they followed Burton to the office on the right side of the factory. "Is this the whole site?" she asked, taking it all in.

"We have another plant in Telford." He threw the answer over his shoulder as he wedged the office door open and showed them inside. "The Telford plant takes care of English orders. We supply Wales."

"I see." Yvonne sat in the seat he had pulled out for her, in front of a busy desk.

Dewi sat next to the DI.

Kevin Burton switched on a kettle in the corner and

readied three mugs. "How can we help you?" he asked, spooning instant into each vessel. "I'm guessing this is about what happened to Jon Tudor's wife?"

"It is..." The DI took out her notebook. "And to ask you about Jonathan, and what you all do here at the plant?"

Burton stirred the mugs before handing them to the detectives. "Fire away," he said. "If it helps, I'll tell you all I can."

"I understand you are a chemical distribution firm?"

He nodded. "We have a secure site here, hold a licence to distribute hazardous and non-hazardous chemicals, and can carry out COSHH assessments where needed. That stands for Care Of Substances Hazardous to Health," he added.

"Thank you." The DI saw no reason to point out their awareness of COSHH. "Do you take regular inventories at the plant?"

"We do monthly stock takes, and compare them with the levels expected on our system. The next one is due sometime next week." He cocked his head. "Why do you ask?"

"I wondered whether you could tell us if items were missing? Unaccounted for?"

"Mistakes do creep in on the system, but we can usually find and correct them after a stock take, yes. We carry out extra checks on the most hazardous chemicals."

"At your last stock take, did you find anything missing?"

"I think we found a couple of discrepancies. I am pretty sure we got to the root of those and ironed them out." He narrowed his eyes. "What has this got to do with Jonathan?"

"It may have nothing to do with him, but his wife may have died because of chemical contamination in the park. That is not for public knowledge, however, until we are sure of our facts."

"I saw the incident on the news. I wondered what could have happened... That was a terrible business. I felt awful for Jon. He has two young children as well. It cannot be easy for them without their mother."

Yvonne cleared her throat. "Because of the delicate nature of the event, I cannot go into details regarding the chemicals we believe were involved yet. However, we would appreciate you informing us of any discrepancies in the last and the next chemical stock take. Is that something you could do?"

"Of course." He sat back, scratching his head through thinning brown hair. "Do you think someone stole the chemicals from here and used them in the park?"

"We don't know, and it is only one of our lines of enquiry."

"Do you think Jonathan Tudor was involved in what happened?"

The DI held up her hands. "We are merely covering all angles, and are here because Mr Tudor works for your chemical company. We are covering all bases to ensure we miss nothing. It would be remiss of us not to check this out. It doesn't mean we believe Jon is guilty of anything."

"I see." He nodded, sipping his coffee. "So you would like details of anything we find missing?"

"We would, and the information will go to a specialist unit who will then contact you for specific details and may wish to carry out tests at your premises."

"Of course... What happens if they show the chemicals used in the attack came from our factory?" His brow furrowed in concern. "Would they shut us down for a time? Could we all be under suspicion?"

"We would question you as the site manager, and also Mr Tudor."

"This sounds very serious." He swallowed.

"Two people died, and it left several others seriously ill in the hospitals. Some are still recovering. It was frightening and affected many other people to a lesser extent. We do not know where the chemicals came from. This is only one angle we are investigating. I should put your mind at rest by saying we have several others."

"Thank goodness..." He blew air through his teeth. "When would you like our stock-take details?"

"As soon as possible... I realise that means bringing forward your next inventory, but we need those checks as soon as we can have them."

"Understood."

"How had Mr Tudor been over the last few months?"

He shrugged. "I hadn't noticed a change in him, if that is what you mean? He worked well, as always. Maybe he was a little more cheerful? I often hear him whistling about the place, or singing. He has always done that, but I think he had been doing it more so, over the previous months. Honestly, he seemed happy prior to his wife's death."

"How about his relationships with other colleagues? How had those been?"

"I had no complaints, and I didn't notice a change in how he interacted with me. Everyone gets on here."

"Did he mention his wife, or their relationship at all?"

"Only in passing... The staff and I usually catch up over a cuppa, and the banter had been the usual stuff. He didn't mention arguments or other difficulties. I believe he told us he was taking the family to the Eisteddfod in Newtown. He seemed to look forward to it and said his children would enjoy it. Nothing else stands out, really. I don't see him as the type of person who would poison others. I would be shocked to find out he was the one who harmed people."

"Well, as I said, this is only one line of enquiry, and we have several others. Mr Tudor may be perfectly innocent, and I hope he is."

She stood. "We've taken up enough of your time, Mr Burton. Thank you for your help."

"My pleasure..." He got up from his chair. "I'll see you both out."

"WHAT DO YOU THINK?" Dewi asked as they made their way back to the car.

"Nothing jumps out at me." Yvonne opened her door. "We'll see what the inventory throws up."

13

CONTAMINATION

Damien Lloyd's forehead furrowed. "I can't believe you have asked me here again. How can I run an environmental charity when you are asking me to come here every five minutes?" He placed his hands on his hips, as the DI led him towards an interview room.

"That is a bit of an exaggeration, Mr Lloyd." The DI pulled a face. "This is only the second time we have met you. Please, take a seat."

She pointed to the chair on the opposite side of the desk, as she took her place next to Dewi, organising her papers and the still images taken from CCTV footage.

He leaned back in his chair, arms folded. He was wearing a navy-blue hooded sweater on this occasion, with the hood down.

"How are things with the charity?" she asked. "Is Climactic still accruing followers?"

"It is. We are one of the fastest growing organisations in the country. Our social media is exploding. People care about their kids' future."

"Oh, I don't doubt it." Yvonne nodded. "I think all of us

care about the planet, but not all of us are disruptive activists."

"So why am I here?"

"We wanted to talk to you about the day of the Eisteddfod again. We wanted to go over some things we need clarifying."

He tutted. "Yet more clarification..."

"You know we found chemicals on your leaflets?"

"Sure... Somebody obviously sprayed them or something. I can't help it if some nutcase harms people by covering our leaflets with something obnoxious. How could I have foreseen or prevented that? Maybe the attackers dislike environmental groups. We do seem to pick up enemies when we protest. Some people do not care about the greater good." He flicked his head in disgust. "They are probably laughing about you questioning me again. It has probably given the perpetrator a thrill. A good way to get revenge on us — poison our stuff and put us in the frame for the attack."

"Your leaflets contained only one component of the toxin." The DI rubbed her chin. "Did you spend much time at the stall?"

"I went to it once or twice." He frowned. "Why?"

"What were you wearing that day?"

He unfolded his arms. "Christ! I don't know... Er, jeans and a hoodie, I guess... It's what I usually wear."

"What colour was the hoodie?"

He ran a hand through his hair. "Grey? I think I wore a grey one."

"Is this you?" She pushed one of the still images towards him. It showed the figure in front of the Climactic stall at the Eisteddfod. "Take a good look. Is that you with your hood up, and your back towards the camera?"

He shrugged. "It could be, from what I can see. There's a few people at the front of the photo. It's difficult to see past them."

"But you think it could be you?"

"Maybe?"

Yvonne placed the other stills alongside, such that they were in a row; depicting movement as the figure appeared to take something out of the front of his top or place something inside it. "Have a look at the images. What do you see? What is the hooded figure doing, would you say?"

"That is not me." He flicked at the photos.

"But you just told us you thought it might be you?"

"Yeah, but I didn't do any of that."

"Any of what?"

"Acting suspicious."

"When you say acting suspicious, what do you mean?"

"Well, that guy is doing something at our stall. I don't know what, but I'd say he is stealing something, or putting something on our table. That wasn't me. I checked on the stall, but I didn't linger there. I let Gary do all the leaflet stuff."

"Do you know your height?"

He shrugged. "Five-ten, five-eleven... They have measured me as both in the past."

"And you're fairly athletic?"

"I work out. You need to be reasonably strong when you are protesting. We get pushed around a lot, you know? Having a bit of meat on you helps with resistance. And it makes us heavier to carry, when you lot come to move us on. I use alfalfa to boost my protein levels."

"Because you are vegan?"

"Right."

"The figure in this footage is around five-eleven, so that

would fit with you. And it is clear he has good-sized muscles."

"Well, I know that fits me, but I'm pretty sure that isn't me. Like I said, I didn't fiddle about at the table like that. The man in those pictures is someone else." He tossed his head. "Even if it was me, how would you prove it from those? This isn't evidence of anything."

"Are you suggesting you did something wrong, but we don't have the evidence in these photographs?"

"Look, I told you, that isn't me. I push boundaries. I have to. It's what environmental campaigners do. But I do not poison people to make a point. Why would I? How does poisoning the environment help our cause? It doesn't, that's how."

"Our specialist officers will need access to your headquarters."

"You mean my flat?"

"If that is your headquarters?"

"Well, we don't have any other."

"Then they will require access to your flat."

"I think it isn't necessary, but they can come and look over my place anytime."

"I'll let them know that."

"You do that." He pursed his lips, defiance in his fiery eyes and the way he jutted his out his chin.

"We are not your enemy, Damien. People died after being in the park that day, and it is our job to find out how and why."

"Well, you would be better at your job if you stopped chasing me."

The DI pressed her lips together. "Thank you. We'll bear that in mind."

~

If Anne Edward's eyes had been pistols, both Yvonne and Dewi would be riddled with holes.

The detectives exchanged glances as she hung her jacket over the back of her chair in the interview room, before glaring at them, arms folded; lips pressed firmly together.

"Thank you for coming in, Ms Edwards. I realise this is the second time we have spoken to you. We know how busy you are and hope not to keep you for too long."

The woman jutted out her chin. "I don't know what I can tell you, that I haven't already said."

Yvonne cocked her head. "I understand, but we have specific questions to put to you." She cleared her throat when there was no reply from the woman staring at her in defiance. "It is about the Eisteddfod, specifically your stall, on the day of the attack."

Edwards shrugged.

"How well do you know Damien Lloyd?"

The woman frowned. "I've known Damien for years. Why?"

"How much time did you spend with him that day?"

"Well, we travelled to Newtown together. He picked me up on the way there."

"What about once you had set up your stall?"

"I saw him on and off after that."

"What was he wearing?"

Her frown deepened, and she scratched her head. "I think he was wearing a dark hoodie... Might have been grey? I think it was grey, yes. And jeans, if I recall correctly?"

"Did he have his hood up or down?"

"Down... What is this?"

"Did he put it up at all?"

"Not when he was with me... But, I suppose the sun was beating down, and he may have covered his head to shade it. But, honestly? I didn't see him with his hood up at any point."

"Would you have noticed if he had?"

"It would have stuck out to me, yes."

Yvonne leaned back, her eyes on Anne Edward's face. "Forensics have been analysing the toxic chemicals that caused people to fall sick during the festival."

"Okay..."

"They found your leaflets positive for one component."

Anne Edwards's mouth fell open. "What? Are you being serious?"

"I am. We tested multiple leaflets and found all of them contained the chemical."

"Bloody hell!" The woman whistled through pursed lips. "That is crazy. Does Damien know?"

"We spoke to him about it."

"Well, what did he say? Did he know about it?"

"He said he didn't know until we told him."

Anne shook her head, her eyes once again spitting defiance. "We're being set up. We're being framed for whatever went down."

"Who do you think would want to frame you?" the DI asked.

"You don't bring about change without making a few enemies along the way. I bet there are a few outfits that would gladly see us hauled through the courts."

"Has anyone else threatened you?"

"Many a time..."

"Recently?"

"All the time... People get angry with us because of our

disruptive tactics. But if we don't upset things, no-one pays attention."

"You can't force people to support you." Yvonne kept her voice even. "They either do, or they don't."

"Most folks are not as clued up as they should be about the environment. They put their short-term interests in front of the planet's long-term future."

"They have lives to live, and your disruptive tactics sometimes stop pregnant women and sick people getting to a hospital."

"Well, that is the sort of disruption that gets noticed. Otherwise, we're just like flies buzzing around the place and being ignored."

The DI smiled at the analogy.

"What's funny?" Edwards glared at Yvonne.

"I wondered why you referred to yourselves as flies."

"Some people see us as a pain, and they want it all to go away. They will be in a great deal more agony as the planet overheats."

"Coming back to Damien..." Yvonne raised a brow.

"He is someone who cares. I will not help you trash his reputation."

"I am not trying to rubbish anybody's reputation, but I need to know who made all those festival-goers sick."

"Damien has good intentions."

"That may be, but he printed those leaflets and took them to the Eisteddfod. They subsequently tested positive for an ingredient of the toxin that was spread in the park."

"Yeah, well, someone probably put the poison on them, or swapped contaminated ones for our non-contaminated ones. Have you thought of that?"

It had crossed the DI's mind that the hooded man may have been there to swap the leaflets. Perhaps someone had swapped them for contaminated ones later that day to perpetrate the attack mid-afternoon, when the most people would be in the park. She put this to Edwards.

"Do you know how desperate you sound?" The woman narrowed her eyes. "You lot are unbelievable."

"Maybe you swapped the leaflets?"

"Don't you dare try fitting me up for this? You'll be planting evidence next."

"We don't manufacture evidence, Anne." Yvonne's gaze was steady. "We search for the truth. You don't get to truth by planting evidence."

"Well, I wouldn't put chemicals on leaflets."

"You've egged MPs before." The DI peered down at her notes. "Frequently."

"Eggs don't make anyone sick."

"People can have an allergy to eggs?"

Edwards tutted.

"And you have daubed banks and other buildings with yellow paint."

"Paint is harmless."

"It costs money, and energy, to remove it. Energy which impacts the environment."

"What has this got to do with contaminated leaflets?"

"It shows you are not averse to using substances to make an impact."

"Yeah, harmless substances."

"Nevertheless..."

Edwards held out her wrists. "Guess you got me, then. Might as well take me down now."

"No need to be facetious, Ms Edwards," Dewi warned.

"I'm asking. I am not accusing you, Anne." Yvonne sighed. "If we do not find the person or persons who did this, they may very well do it again. It could be you or your loved ones in the firing line next time. Do you not see that?"

Anne lowered her eyes. "I get it, but I honestly did not see Damien with his hood up at any point. Then again, I wasn't with him the whole time. We are not joined at the hip. And I do not say that to be facetious." She cast a glance at Dewi. "It's just the way it is."

"And, are you saying you know nothing about how the chemical came to be on your organisation's leaflets?"

"That is exactly what I am saying. I don't know how it came to be on them, and I was not responsible."

"Very well." The DI put her pen down. "We won't keep you any longer."

"I'm free to go?"

"Of course."

"Right." Anne Edwards looked at her watch. "I'll be off. I hope you won't be needing me again."

"We make no promises." Yvonne smiled. "But I hope that for you, too."

14

STOLEN SHIPMENT

Septtember arrived, accompanied by wind and heavy rain, as leaves began turning the vibrant colours of senescence.

Yvonne stared through the windows in CID over the trees in Dolerw park where the attack had taken place a month earlier.

The phone ringing disturbed her from her thoughts. She headed over to her desk to answer it. "Yvonne Giles..."

"Hi it's Kevin Burton, the manager at Kemikal."

"Ah, hello, Kevin." She checked her watch. It was eleven o'clock. "What can I do for you?"

"We have been through our stock, and nothing appears to be missing."

"I see..." She couldn't help feeling disappointed at the news. Another lead gone. Or was it?

"However, you should know that we had part of a shipment go missing eighteen months ago. I realise it may be irrelevant to your inquiry, because of the time involved, but I thought you ought to know anyway, so you have the complete picture."

She frowned in concentration. "When you say part of a shipment, what are we talking about?"

"Someone broke into one of our containers and took approximately a fifth of its load. The chemicals were being transported by lorry from a manufacturing plant in Scotland to our warehouse near Shrewsbury. We believe someone planned the theft and specifically targeted our shipment."

"And what were the circumstances of the theft?"

"It was from one of our overnight transports. The driver parked in a lay-by while he rested and grabbed refreshment. He left the lorry for half an hour while he visited a truck stop and, when he got back, the container was gone. Someone must have known that the driver stopped in that lay by when he was doing the overnight haulage of our chemicals."

"Can you provide a record of what thieves took?"

"We can."

"Would you be so kind as to email or fax it through to us? The details are on the card I gave you, if you still have it?"

"I do, and we will. Both police Scotland and West Mercia Police handled the case, because of where the theft took place, and where our stock was being taken."

"Great, we can liaise with them." Yvonne noted this down. "Were the thieves found? Did you locate your chemicals?"

"No one caught the thieves, and we didn't recover our stock."

"I see... Thank you for this information, Mr Burton. If you can fax us the details as soon as possible, we can investigate whether the missing chemicals could have anything to do with our case."

"No problem."

Yvonne put down the phone.

"Was that Kemikal?" Dai asked, handing her a mug of tea.

"Thank you, yes. They had part of a chemical shipment stolen eighteen months ago. They are faxing through details of the missing substances. Could you grab the fax when it comes through and relay the details to the NCA? Ask them if any of the stolen chemicals could have any relevance to our case."

"Will do."

"You may need to liaise with the Scottish police and West Mercia to find out what they learned about the incident."

"Got it." He rolled his sleeves up.

"Thanks, Dai."

THE FOLLOWING DAY, Yvonne tapped on DCI Llewelyn's door.

He had asked to see her, and she knew he would want to know if they had solid leads, and a decent suspect. She steeled herself, ready for the disappointment that would inevitably come when she admitted the case was still wide open.

She poked her head around the door. "You wanted to see me, sir?"

"Yvonne... Yes, I asked to see you. Please, take a seat." He finished collating some papers and stapled them, setting them aside before pushing his glasses up onto his head. "I wanted to know whether we have made any progress towards an arrest for the chemical spill in the park?"

"Don't you mean chemical attack, sir?" She raised her brows.

"Have we proved it was deliberate?" He leaned back in his chair.

"I believe that leaflets being infused with one ingredient of nerve agent would suggest it was, sir, yes."

"I am inclined to agree, making an imminent arrest even more important. Wouldn't you say?"

"I would." Yvonne ran a hand through her hair as she took a seat. "I would also say we are making progress, but an arrest is not yet on the cards."

"Why not?" He cocked his head.

"We have identified several suspects, Chris, and are working to rule them in or out. There are several lines of enquiry, and these things take time."

He sighed. "Anything promising? You know I am under pressure from the chief constable and crime commissioner?"

"I do, and I can promise you we are working as fast as we can on this."

"Okay..."

"We are liaising with Police Scotland and West Mercia regarding theft of chemicals from a lorry shipment eighteen months ago. The NCA have confirmed that some of the missing chemicals were consistent with the ingredients of the nerve agent which affected people during the Eisteddfod. So we are very keen to find out who perpetrated the theft. The heist was well-planned and appeared to have inside knowledge regarding movements of the shipment and habits of the lorry driver. Timing was critical for the theft, as the driver parked in the lay-by for an hour at most."

"Have we spoken to the company from which the chemicals were stolen?"

"We have. In fact, they contacted us regarding the former theft. It is a company from Shrewsbury, known as Kemikal. We had already spoken to them. The husband of a female victim of the Newtown attack who died, Charlene Tudor, works for the company. His name is Jonathan Tudor. Charlene's sister informed us he was having an affair, and that he worked for Kemikal."

"Could he have been the inside man?" Llewelyn rubbed his chin.

"That is what I have been pondering this afternoon, whether he might have perpetrated the theft himself, or helped someone else, and kept back some of the booty to use on his wife."

"Is there any credence to the assertion he was having an affair?"

The DI nodded. "He denied it to us at first, but Charlene's sister photographed him making out with a woman in his car. Charmaine took the pictures from her own vehicle. We put the photos to him, and he eventually admitted the affair. However, he denies wanting to harm his wife."

"You said you had others in mind for the theft, too?"

"We do. They include the leaders of the environmental group, Climactic, because their handouts tested positive for one of the chemical reagents used in the attack; a local previously convicted for growing cannabis, and who had sent threatening letters to town dignitaries; and a property mogul who the council refused to sell parkland to. He was desperate to buy part of Dolerw to develop as an entertainment and restaurant complex."

"And you are following all of those leads up?"

"We are, yes."

"It sounds like you have your hands full, and I can see you are getting on with things. I won't keep you, Yvonne, but please keep me informed. Remember, we are under pressure on this. I know you will work as quickly as you can."

"I will, sir." She nodded. "We hope to have a breakthrough soon."

"I'm glad to hear it. Thank you, Yvonne. I know I can count on you and your team."

"Thank you, sir."

As she left the DCI's office, the DI crossed her fingers.

15

THE LORRY IN THE LAY-BY

"I can't believe you want to interview me again." Jonathan Tudor scowled. "I lost my wife because of whatever took place in that park. And here you are, demanding my time, when I am trying to put my own and my children's lives back together. Have you no heart?"

Yvonne pressed her lips tight. She understood his frustration. If she were in his shoes, and innocent of any involvement in the park attack, she would also feel indignant. But they had uncovered several connections between Tudor and the chemical event. And Porton Down had confirmed that the chemical signatures of the compounds used in the attack matched those stolen from the Kemikal shipment. The circumstantial evidence was mounting. "I understand your feelings." The DI motioned for him to take a seat once they reached the interview room. "And believe me, I feel the intrusion as acutely as yourself. I know it is a sensitive time for you, Mr Tudor. But, until we have the answers to our questions, we cannot push forward with our investigation into what happened in the park. The reasons your wife lost her life that day."

Yvonne's explanation quieted him, and he sat as requested.

"Thank you." She said, her voice soft. "We asked you here today because we received confirmation that the substances used to poison people in Dolerw came from Kemikal, the company you work for."

He brought his eyes to hers, his forehead furrowed. "What?"

Porton Down carried out extensive testing and confirmed the chemical signatures were identical to those in one of your shipments. Part of a Kemikal cargo that was stolen eighteen months ago.

He scratched his head. "I remember that... they broke into one of our lorries and stole some chemicals."

"Yes."

"And you have traced the park poison back to that shipment?"

"Yes."

"Wow..." He sat back, running a hand through his hair. "I'm trying to get my head around that," he said.

"I'll give you a minute." Yvonne nodded, exchanging glances with Dewi.

"I can't believe Charlene died because of chemicals from our company." He sighed, shaking his head. "That was not even on my radar."

"Can you see, now, why we would want to speak with you again?"

"I realise this doesn't look good... But I know nothing of the theft of items from our shipment, and my wife's death was the last thing I expected when I took my family to the Eisteddfod."

"Going back to the night of the theft, eighteen months ago, we know the driver parked in the lay-by for only thirty minutes. That is a brief window for such a theft. Don't you think?"

He shrugged. "Opportunists can strike anywhere, can't they?" Beads of sweat formed on his temples.

"Sure, but not only did the break-in occur in that time-frame, but they took specific substances that I am told are fairly innocuous and odd items for a theft... unless the thief knew how they could utilise them? It was as though the perpetrators had a specific use in mind."

He shrugged. "Maybe they did... How does that relate to me?"

"You were engaging in an affair about which you lied to us. And your wife is dead because of chemicals stolen from your place of employment. That is how this relates to you. It doesn't make you guilty, but it begs questions for which we would like answers."

"Fine... Go ahead; ask me. Aside from the affair, I have a clear conscience." He shifted position in his chair.

"Very well... Did you ever discuss with anyone details of shipments for your company? Modes of transport, for example, or the process involved? Did you tell anyone who the drivers were, and what hours they liked to keep?"

"You mean before the theft took place?"

"Yes... prior to the heist."

"Not that I recall. I mean, I had no need to. I can't imagine who I would talk to about that." A pearl of sweat ran down the side of his face.

"Did you know the driver's movements? The routes and break times?"

"Not to the precise minute... I mean, I don't think our drivers go around telling people what time they take a break. They just do it, as far as I know. Someone breaking into one of our lorries during the driver's refreshment break? In a lay-by? They would have to have been following the vehicle, or lying in wait, hoping the driver stop somewhere convenient. Personally? I bet they followed the lorry. They had to have done."

"Did you follow the vehicle?"

He screwed his face up. "No."

"Did you tail the lorry and steal from it?"

"Certainly not."

"Perhaps you planned your wife's demise many months before the attack."

"How many more times? I neither planned nor wanted my wife's death. Whatever you may think of me for having an affair, I did not plan to harm my wife. You know, most people who have affairs are much more likely to give up on the extra-marital relationship than their marriage. It's a fact. Look it up."

"But some do."

"That may be... But, I didn't." He shifted position.

"Are you still seeing the other woman?"

"I have seen her, yes. I don't feel proud of myself, but losing Charlene... I need someone to talk to, someone who understands, and a confidant I can discuss the children with; seek advice. Charlene used to do the household stuff and see to the children's lunches for school and any other needs. It is all new to me. Debbie advises me. She is a kind shoulder, when I have no other. I don't see my family very often. I have always prided myself on being independent. Charlene's loss has taught me that sometimes we really need others in our lives. This is one of them. I told you, I loved my wife. Affair or not, I miss her daily. I wish she hadn't left."

"She died."

"Fine, then I wish she hadn't died. If I could have her

back tomorrow, I would." He took out a hanky and mopped his forehead.

"You seem uncomfortable, Mr Tudor." Dewi's deep voice intervened.

"This line of questioning is making me uncomfortable." He glared at the DS. "You imagine... You take your wife and kids to the park for a day out. One minute, you are standing with the children; waiting for your wife to bring you a beer, and the next you are watching her and many others fighting for breath. I know you are investigating the horror, but I lived it. Have some compassion. Try to see it from my point of view. Tell me you have other suspects. Please tell me there are others you are investigating. I want my wife's murder solved. I need that. My children need it. Maybe not now. They are too young to fully understand, but when they are older, they will have so many questions. I want them to have the answers to why this happened."

"There are other lines of enquiry." Yvonne nodded. "And we are thoroughly investigating those, too. You can rest assured of that."

"Good." He nodded. "Can I go now? Only, I have to pick the children up from school."

"Of course." Yvonne pushed her chair back from the table. "I'll see you out."

BACK IN THE OFFICE, Callum and Dai had been waiting for Yvonne and Dewi to return.

Callum approached them both. "We've been looking into the stolen chemicals theft eighteen months ago."

"Great, and?" Yvonne perched on the end of the nearest desk to listen.

"Kemikal was subject to protests from several environmental groups, including Climactic."

"Really?"

Dai joined them. "Yes... The groups protested that recently banned pesticides were still being manufactured by the firm, albeit in reduced amounts. The company protested they were for legitimate purposes, but Climactic and others pushed back, saying they believed there was no legitimate reason for them to still be producing the compounds."

Callum nodded. "Kemikal was not doing anything wrong, but the protests carried on for several months."

The DI frowned. "So we come back to the likes of Damien Lloyd and Anne Edwards?"

"The biggest bombshell is they were staking out delivery routes, and had stopped several chemical and petrochemical lorries. They had the motive and the opportunity."

"The lay-by..." Yvonne ran a hand through her mussed locks. "Wow, well done, lads."

"Thanks..." Callum placed his hands on his hips. "If anyone was going to know where the shipments were, it would have been those environmental groups."

"Superb work, guys." Dewi gave Callum a pat on the back. "I owe you a pint."

16

POISONOUS CONNECTIONS

Yvonne stared through the window of CID at the trees swaying in the wind around Dolerw Park. She was alone in the office, being the first to arrive that morning. She sipped hot coffee but, in her mind's eye, she could see the stretchers; the fear, and people running through the carpark into the streets on the day everything changed for the town.

Acutely aware they had not yet identified the perpetrators of the attack, she allowed her mind to pour over the information they had gathered so far. Tasha's words came back to her, and the psychologist's suggestion that an individual as opposed to a group contaminated the Eisteddfod. And that the action could have been revenge for a perceived wrong, or an attempt to shock the community for a reason unlikely to be linked to terror. So what exactly were they looking at?

"Damien Lloyd is here." Dewi broke her reverie as he threw his jacket over the back of his chair. "I said I would pass on the message. Do you want me with you?"

"Yes, I would like you there, Dewi." She nodded. "This

could be a difficult one. I'll be asking him about the protests his group carried out at Kemikal last year and the theft of the shipment. It could get hairy."

"Right you are, Yvonne. I'll just grab a coffee. I was stuck in traffic this morning after an accident on the bypass." He sighed. "It's typical, when I have a lot on."

She cocked her head. "Are you sure you have the time for this interview?"

"Absolutely..." He grinned. "I just need some caffeine first."

DAMIEN LLOYD WAS AS PLEASED AS EVER to be back at the Newtown police station. He sat back in his chair, arms folded; legs stretched and crossed at the ankles. The hood of his sweatshirt was up over his head, and it was obvious he would not speak until spoken to.

The DI took a deep breath as she sat.

Dewi seemed relaxed as he settled next to her.

Yvonne spread her papers in front as though about to ask someone to pick a card. Any card. "Thank you for coming in again, Damien. I realise you are a busy man, and we hope this will not take too long."

"I don't know what I can tell you I haven't already said." His eyes were on the table.

"Would you like to take your hood down? It is hard to talk to someone when you cannot see their face."

"Fine." He pulled at it roughly, mussing his hair as the material slid from his head.

"That's better..." She smiled, attempting to warm the decidedly chilly atmosphere.

"So, why ask me here again? Have you got more dodgy

footage of a man dressed vaguely the same as me with his back to the camera?" He looked up, his eyes meeting hers. "Has there been another chemical spill you need a patsy for?"

"There's no need for that." She pressed her lips together.

He sighed. "Then tell me why I am here."

"Twelve months ago, your eco warrior group, Climactic, were protesting outside of a chemical plant and distribution centre. Do you remember that?"

He shrugged. "We've protested outside of a few. You'll have to be specific."

"A plant called Kemikal, near Shrewsbury. Ring any bells, now?"

"Vaguely."

"Well, do you remember, *vaguely*, spraying yellow paint over the entrance doors of the plant?"

"I didn't do the painting at Kemikal. I've daubed other places, but I didn't do that one."

"Were you there?"

"I might have popped down occasionally."

"Have you ever attacked that plant in other ways?"

He narrowed his eyes. "What do you mean?"

"Around the same time that Climactic and other groups were protesting the site, Kemikal had chemicals stolen in what seemed a well-planned heist."

His face darkened. "I wouldn't know anything about that."

"Your group was the most vociferous during the protests, apparently. Climactic were high on the company's suspect list."

"The West Mercia Police interviewed us while they were investigating the theft. They were satisfied we had no involvement."

"Yes well, our officers are liaising with West Mercia and Police Scotland as we speak."

"Good for them." He tossed his head. "They'll soon find out we had nothing to do with it."

"It is a notable coincidence, though, wouldn't you say?"

"Oh, it must be us then... I should confess right now."

"Did your group have any involvement in the theft from a Kemikal transport lorry en route to England from Scotland?"

"No."

"Have you ever stolen chemicals?"

"I stole some alcohol from the school chemistry lab once, but didn't get very far with it. They caught me in the corridor and marched me to the headmaster's office by my ear."

The DI pressed her lips together.

Damien's glare softened. "Look, I know you think we spread the contamination in the park, but we didn't. I keep telling you. It wasn't us. We do things to get attention, sure. But hurting people? That really isn't our thing."

"Newspapers reported you as stating you would disrupt the company's business by any means?"

He sighed. "I may have said that in the heat of the moment, but I didn't mean stealing their cargo."

"What did you mean?"

He looked down at the table. "There are other ways."

"What other ways?"

"Well, what we were doing... protesting outside of the factory, giving it a lick of paint. I think other groups may have hacked their systems. We didn't. And we didn't steal their stock."

Yvonne leaned back in her chair, unsure whether Lloyd was telling the truth. For now, however, she couldn't keep him. "Very well. There are no more questions today. But be aware, we have our eye on your organisation, and what you are getting up to."

"Fine, but, as far as I know, protesting is still legal in our country."

"You have a right to protest, but you do not have a right to break the law. I would thank you for bearing that in mind."

~

BACK IN THE OFFICE, the DI approached Callum and Dai. "Did you find any connection between Climactic and the Kemikal heist? Could they have been involved in the theft?"

Dai shook his head. "We have found nothing so far. Nothing to tie Damien Lloyd or Climactic to the heist. They protested at the main plant, but there is nothing which puts them in Scotland, or even the north of England, when the theft took place."

"Okay..." She nodded. "For completeness, I think you should check the other environmental groups who were protesting around the same time. Investigate whether any of them have connections to the town, or motive for the attack on the Eisteddfod."

"Will do, ma'am."

~

WEDNESDAY MORNING BEGAN with an unblemished sky as Yvonne left the house. But, by the time she had completed the half-hour drive to work, black clouds had gathered and given the air a cool, damp feel.

The DI pondered the case, and who might have been

responsible for the chemical contamination at the Eisteddfod. Every single one of their suspects insisted they had nothing to do with it. Although Damien Lloyd's leaflets might be considered a smoking gun, it could have been anyone responsible for spraying the piles as they lay on the table that day. Poor visibility through the crowds had made it impossible to identify the hooded figure at Climactic's stall seen on camera footage. And they could not be sure whether the crime was a one-off attack on the festival, or only the first of several planned. Her head ached from worrying about it.

She was still ruminating on this as she entered the station.

The duty sergeant called her over. "I thought you should know that Kevin Mills, leader of the town council, has received a threatening letter. I bagged it up and gave it to Dewi a minute ago."

The DI's brow furrowed. "Did Councillor Mills come in here?"

"He did, ma'am, but he said he had a meeting to attend. He left the letter with me."

"Did he say when he received it?"

"Yesterday evening, when he returned from work. It looks like they posted it in Shrewsbury. The envelope is with the letter."

"I see... Well, thank you for letting me know. I'll look at it when I get upstairs."

Dewi had a cuppa waiting for her. "Thought you might appreciate that. The morning has turned decidedly cold."

"Thank you for the tea, Dewi. You are a star." She put her jacket over the back of her chair. "I hear you have the letter that was sent to the leader of the council?"

"To Kevin Mills? Yes, it's on my desk. I was going to let

you settle in before I told you about it. Mills said the postal worker delivered it yesterday. He found it when he got home and brought it in this morning."

"We should get it to forensics for testing," she said, donning latex gloves. "I'll have a quick look before we get it off to them."

Dewi brought her the letter in a sealed, transparent evidence bag. "The sender doesn't say what he plans on doing, but says he will make the councillor regret his actions."

"Hmm..." She frowned, reading the note. "The sender is not a happy bunny."

"You can say that again." Dewi grinned. "It's typed, so we don't have the perp's handwriting, but we may get a fingerprint or two from it."

"It looks laser-printed."

"The sender was cautious." Dewi nodded.

"And sent from Shrewsbury? They may have travelled there to disguise where they live."

The DS rubbed his neck. "Judging by the sentiments in the letter, I think they must be a local. As you can see, it talks about decisions made by the councillor. He evidently upset them."

Yvonne rubbed her chin. "I wonder if Hywel Owen has been up to his old tricks? Wasn't Mills, the councillor who reported Owen for growing cannabis? When you get this off to forensics, can you ask them to compare it with the letters he sent previously? I am talking about the language used, because he wrote his previous letters by hand." She snapped a photograph with her mobile. "We can pull Owen's old letters up on the system, and do a rough comparison ourselves, but I'd like forensics to study them both thoroughly."

"No problem."

"WHAT DO YOU THINK?" Yvonne peered at the copies of Owen's old letters on her screen. "There are similarities, but they are not identical in style." She straightened up. "What are your thoughts, Dewi?"

"I think there's enough there to warrant a discussion with Mr Owen."

"Agreed." She nodded. "Owen's original letter talked about making the council pay. I think we should get him in; see what he has to say for himself. My only reservation involves the language used. This new letter is more formal in style than Owen's previous ones. Ideally, we should wait until forensics has done a proper comparison, but I am worried the Eisteddfod perpetrator might attack again. I think we should interview him now and either rule him in or out. If he wrote this letter, he will think twice about acting on it if he knows we are into him."

17

A WAY WITH WORDS

Hywel Owen sat with his arms folded; hair neatly slicked over the top of his head; his belly straining the material of his waistcoat a little less this time.

"Thank you for joining us again, Mr Owen." Yvonne placed her pen on her paperwork as she introduced the two of them and Dewi for the recording. "I'm sure you are wondering why we asked you in again?"

"I assumed you were still trying to set me up for the incident at the Eisteddfod... Trying to make me fit the criminal profile." He unfolded his arms, stretching them out in front of him. "Well, you might as well get on with it and ask me what you want."

"Do you remember the letter you tried to send to Kevin Mills from prison last year?"

He frowned. "Well, I'm not likely to forget, am I? They gave me extra time inside for it. And I got a dressing down from the governor."

"Did you try again three days ago?"

"What?" He frowned.

"Did you type a threatening letter to Councillor Mills and post it three days ago?"

"No, I did not. Why would I?"

"Because you did it before, and you might still be angry about him reporting you to police?"

"I'm not so sad that I would still be mulling all that rubbish. I have better things to do. Has somebody threatened him for real?"

"Yes, they have."

"Obviously, he pissed someone else off as well." He laughed.

"You find that funny?"

"Well, I won't cry about someone else sending him a nasty letter, no way. The man tried to ruin my life."

"He didn't wreck your life," Yvonne corrected. "He reported you because you committed a criminal offence. Don't you think it was you who was ruining your own life by planning to sell drugs?"

"I told you I was growing it for personal consumption."

"The amount you had? Two hundred plants, and some already harvested? Really? You would have been permanently off your face."

"Maybe that's the way I like it." He folded his arms again.

"I thought you said you wanted it for pain relief?"

"That, as well."

The DI cleared her throat. "You have previous for getting revenge on others using poison. As you did with your garage colleagues, who were expecting you to make the tea because you were the youngest employee."

"That has nothing to do with anything."

"What were you planning on doing to Mr Mills?"

"When?"

"When you wrote the threatening letter in prison. What were you planning to do to him? You didn't specify."

"I wasn't really going to act on it, was I? I wasn't really going to harm him. It was more about scaring him, to keep him looking over his shoulder, and afraid of what might come out of the dark."

"And how did you feel when the prison officers discovered your letter?"

"Mostly annoyed and disappointed. I didn't even know if he knew I had sent it. They didn't tell me. I really wanted him to know."

"Given what you have told me, I think you can understand why we would look at you now that Mills has received another letter."

"Yeah, well, I didn't send another one. I wish I had, even though I don't want prison again. But I didn't write it. He must have pissed someone else off, like he did with me."

"Have you always refused to accept responsibility for your behaviour?"

"I didn't send it." He puffed air through his lips.

"I didn't mean that... I meant you blaming your anger on Councillor Mills, instead of facing up to the fact he reported you for committing an offence."

Owen lowered his eyes.

"This latest letter does not specify the threat... Just like the letter you wrote in prison."

He shrugged. "Maybe that is because whoever wrote this latest letter did not really intend doing anything wrong, like I didn't. I left out what I would do because I did not know what to threaten."

"Not poison? Like you did to your former colleagues?"

"Look, you keep dragging that up, but I was young and naïve when I did that. I thought a few drips of weedkiller would make them sick and give them gas. I didn't think they would be as unwell as they were. But they all recovered fine, and it was no harm done in my mind. If I had really wanted to hurt them, I'd have poured in the lot."

The DI shuddered. "That is a little cold, Mr Owen."

"Yes, but the point is, I didn't. I don't go round hurting people, and I was seventeen when I did that poisoning thing. I didn't know enough about life back then, and I freely admit it was wrong. So, I learned my lesson, and have done nothing like it since."

"Where were you three days ago?"

"I was at my home in Llanfair."

"All day?"

"All day."

"No trips to Shrewsbury?"

"I was home."

"Can anyone verify that?"

"I popped into the village tea shop that day, I think? I was helping a farmhand in the morning. Then I popped into the village for some lunch and a pot of tea that I didn't have to make myself."

"And the farmhand and cafe will confirm this if we ask them, will they?"

"Of course."

"Very well." The DI nodded. "We will verify your story and, if it checks out, we will not bother you further."

"I'm relieved to hear it." He sighed. "Look, I have tried to put my past behind me. It's hard, especially when I feel eyes on me when I walk around. Maybe those eyes aren't really there, but I am self-conscious. I brazen it out, but it affects me, as I cannot change the past. The Hywel I was back then was young and foolish, and later I was angry at being in prison. I can be an idiot, I know. But I really want to put it all behind me and have a settled life again. I'm getting old. My body doesn't work as well, and I get pain on and off. This old bugger just wants to be left alone. I didn't poison people in the park, and I didn't threaten Mills again. I may have laughed about it, but I didn't do it. That is all I have to say on the matter."

"Thank you, Mr Owen. You can go. If we need to speak to you again, we will let you know. But we won't unless it is absolutely necessary."

~

THE LETTER SENT to Kevin Mills was back, forensics having confirmed it was absent of fingerprints and DNA. They also asserted that the words and phrases used in the letter differed significantly from those in the letter Hywel Owen wrote while in prison. In their opinion, two distinct individuals wrote the letters.

"So, we're back at square one." Dewi sighed.

Yvonne pursed her lips. "I know it feels like that, but we are making progress." Her eyes were on the letter, her thoughts turning to Kamal Bronson. She called Callum over.

"Everything all right?" he asked.

"Could you ask the council planning department for details of Kamal Bronson's planning application and the reasons they turned it down?"

"Sure."

"And find out whether Kevin Mills was involved in the decision-making."

"Will do." Callum cocked his head. "Your eyes are sparkling... You're onto something..."

She pressed her lips together. "Maybe, Callum... Maybe."

"What are you thinking?" Dewi asked, after Callum had left to make enquiries.

"Bronson is not short on resources. He has the means to pull off a stunt like the chemical heist from Kemikal, and he has a motive for threatening a council member. We also know he is well-spoken, and more likely to use language like that expressed in the letter to Mills. Tasha thinks the park attackers didn't target the Eisteddfod, just the town. She thinks they intended harming people because of a perceived wrong. That had us linking it to Hywel Owen, but it could as likely be Kamal Bronson. And, like I say, he has considerable means at his disposal. I think we should speak to him again. If what Callum gleans from the council is relevant, we should find out Bronson's current whereabouts and question him as soon as possible. Here or at his offices, it doesn't really matter, but I would like to see what he has to say about all this."

Dewi's brow furrowed. "He doesn't have previous, Yvonne."

"I know, but if he wants land in Dolerw that badly, perhaps he would harm people in order to get it. After what happened, others might have changed their minds about investing in the land. If they cancelled their plans, it might have given him a way in."

"Your intuition is usually good." The DS nodded. "It's certainly worth investigating." He waved his notebook at the DI. "Don't forget we have a meeting with Councillor Mills at lunchtime tomorrow. Perhaps he can shed some light on Bronson's plans."

"Thank you for reminding me, Dewi." She grinned. "I had forgotten."

18

DANGER LURKS

They arrived ten minutes late for their meeting with Kevin Mills, at the council offices in Dolerw, and found the councillor absent.

"I'm so sorry, he went out." The receptionist grimaced. "He said to give you his apologies and left right after his last meeting. He seemed in a hurry and said he had to go home."

"Sorry, I don't know your name." The DI tilted her head.

"Tracy," she answered. "Tracy Betts."

"Well, thank you, Tracy. Could we have his address, please?"

"Of course... One moment..." The woman tapped on her keyboard; eventually pushing back her chair. "He lives in Kerry." A loud whirring accompanied a page coming off the printer on the desk next to her. She handed it to them. "Here is the address."

"Thank you." Yvonne smiled. "Can I ask who his last meeting was with?"

"He saw..." The fair-haired, bespectacled Tracy ran a finger down the appointments book. "...Kamal Bronson." She looked up at them. "Does that help at all?"

The detectives exchanged glances.

"Did he say where ~~if~~ he was going straight home?" the DI asked.

"No, I'm afraid he didn't."

Yvonne's forehead furrowed, her thoughts racing. "Which room were they in?"

"They met in Councillor Mills's office."

The DI turned to her sergeant. "Dewi, we need the specialist hazards team out here to test the surfaces in Mills's room as soon as possible."

"I'll make the call."

The receptionist stared wide-eyed at Yvonne.

"It's okay... We are not expecting to find anything. We are doing it as a precaution. I like to cover all bases."

"Right..." The woman appeared unconvinced, but the DI did not have time to reassure her further. "Do you have Councillor Mills's mobile number?"

The receptionist pulled a face.

"I am a police officer," Yvonne reminded her.

"Very well." The woman read it out, as the DI punched the numbers into her phone.

She left the front desk to join Dewi outside, as he finished his call to the station. "Are they coming?"

He nodded. "They are on their way... What are you thinking?"

She pursed her lips. "I'm going to feel very foolish if this is nothing, but I am concerned Kevin Mills may be in immediate danger. I am ringing him now."

Mills did not answer his phone.

The DI left a voicemail, instructing him to call her as soon as he got the message and, if possible, to remain in his vehicle.

"What's happening?" Dewi raised a brow. "Why are you asking him to stay in his car?"

Yvonne cast her eyes around the park. It was peaceful. A few people sat around eating sandwiches, or walking their dogs with small children. It was a serenity in contrast to the chaotic scenes only weeks ago. "I am worried that Bronson may have exposed the councillor to a nerve agent constituent. If I am correct, the second reagent may be in the location Mills is heading for, possibly his home."

"Wow..." The DS frowned. "That's a bit of a leap, isn't it?"

"Maybe... But we know Kamal is not best pleased with the councillor and, if he was the one who sent the letter, I don't see him as a person who makes empty threats."

"But Mills didn't know who sent it."

"That's what he told us..."

"Got you." Dewi nodded. "Well, let's hope the councillor gets back to us soon."

THREE PLASTIC-SUITED SOCO officers arrived at the porticoed entrance to the town hall in Dolerw, carrying various bags and boxes.

"Where do you want us?" the first asked.

"We would like you to test a councillor's office, and the handrails on the stairs approaching it. And need the results expedited... Fast as you can, please? We think there may have been a contamination like the one we saw at the Eisteddfod. A suspect for the park attack may have exposed Councillor Mills's room to a constituent of the nerve agent."

He nodded. "Not a problem... We have a testing kit on hand. THe NCA thought we might need it again. Can we have paramedics on standby with the antidote, in case there is more than one constituent present and one of us becomes ill?"

"We'll contact them immediately." She nodded. "Let me know if there is anything else you need."

His face was a mask as he led his colleagues to the stairs and Councillor Mills' office, directed by the receptionist. Tracy Betts informed other council staff of events via telephone, and they began evacuating the building under strict instruction not to touch anything.

Yvonne waited with Dewi on the grass outside.

The DI pulled her jacket tight, wondering whether her gut instinct was correct. She would feel silly if they found nothing but knew, like the adage, it was better to be safe than sorry.

Crime scene officers set up their equipment near the entrance of the building. Brows furrowed as they donned protective gear before collecting samples from the handrails on the stairs and moving on to other areas in the room. They concentrated on door handles and other surfaces most likely to be touched.

As they performed the tests, Yvonne and Dewi waited with bated breath, minds racing.

"We have a positive result," the first specialist officer announced to them when he finally emerged, his voice muffled by the protective suit and face mask. "You must keep everyone away from the building until we have completed decontamination."

Confirmation of a chemical constituent of the nerve agent sent shivers down the DI's spine. Her suspicion had been correct. Kamal Bronson was now firmly in the frame. She nodded. "Can you test the other councillors' cars for a second constituent? I believe the perp targeted a specific individual, but we can't risk being wrong. And we don't know who may have touched the handrails since they were contaminated. I have to go," she informed him. "We have to find Councillor Mills before the perpetrator exposes him to the other reagent."

A SOCO chimed in, "We must ensure the other councillors remain in a safe location until we've tested them. Are uniformed officers on their way?"

"They are," Dewi confirmed. "I've called for backup."

Yvonne suspected Kevin Mills was in grave danger. She turned to Dewi. "We have to find him. Kamal Bronson may have lured him to a second location." She punched numbers into her mobile.

"Yvonne?" Callum's concerned voice answered.

"Hi, Callum. Can you get a description of Bronson sent to all units and arrange for teams to attend his offices and home address? They should proceed with caution and have hazmats available to them. We think Bronson perpetrated the contamination at the park and is extremely dangerous. I will be available on my mobile to speak to whoever needs me."

"Where are you going?" Callum asked.

"We are heading to Councillor Mills's home. He hasn't been answering his phone, and doesn't appear to have received the voicemails I left for him. We don't know if Bronson is with the councillor, but we are going to the home in case they are there. I'll tell you more later. Please let the DCI know what is happening."

"I'm on it. Be careful, ma'am." Callum disconnected.

Dewi scratched his head. "Tracy Betts had confirmation from a colleague that Mills was going home. If Bronson knows where the councillor lives, he may have contaminated door handles on the property. And I would bet he knows Mills's address. The guy has money. I don't think it would be hard for him to get any information he wanted."

"Exactly, Dewi... We'll go to Mills's home and set up a cordon until scientific officers can swab it. And let's hope the councillor didn't go straight to his house."

She approached Tracy Betts, who was standing nearby with colleagues. "Do you know if Councillor Mills has anyone at home?"

Tracy shook her head. "There won't be anyone there at the moment. His wife works, and his teenage daughter attends school. If he went directly home, he is likely on his own."

"Thank you." Yvonne spoke with the specialist hazards team and requested they have personnel go to the Kerry address as soon as practicable. Then headed back to Dewi. "Let's get to Mills's place and set up the cordon. Phone the station and ask for uniformed officers to meet us there."

"Righty-oh."

19

NEAR MISS

Yvonne and Dewi arrived at Kevin Mills's red-brick, detached Victorian home, and donned two pairs of latex gloves each before approaching the house and knocking on the door to verifying whether anyone was home.

Behind them, several police vehicles arrived with lights but no sirens, and parked along the adjacent road.

When nobody came to the door, the DI and DS exited the garden, asking the arriving officers to erect a broad cordon around the home and watch over it until the specialist team arrived to test for, and deal with, any hazardous contamination.

Yvonne and Dewi walked back to their vehicle to wait for the specialist team and Kevin Mills's arrival.

The DI cast her gaze over the house, and the along the lane where they had parked. "It's quiet here, and not overlooked."

Dewi nodded as he opened his car door. "An ideal place for Bronson to leave the second chemical."

"Exactly." Yvonne pursed her lips. "I think he must have been planning this for a while."

"He likely began hatching schemes when they rejected his proposals for Dolerw."

The DI shuddered. "I will never understand some people."

YVONNE REMINDED herself to breathe as they sat in the car, waiting for Mills and the specialist officers to arrive. She worried about the DCI's reaction if this turned out to be wasted time and resources, but felt it was better to risk humiliation and his displeasure than allow the councillor and his family to be put in harm's way. She was glad of Dewi's presence, and of the uniformed officers who would ensure no-one entered the cordon around the home. The DI was still pondering whether they had done enough when a dark BMW approached them along the lane.

The DI and DS opened their doors simultaneously, stepping out of their vehicle.

While he was still several hundred yards away, Mills exited his car, leaving the door wide open as he ran towards the cordon. "What's going on? What happened?" he asked.

As he shouted this, the door to his house opened, and a young girl with headphones around her neck came out.

"Oh my God, no." Yvonne ran towards Mills. "Stop... Stay where you are."

He didn't hear her, as he and his daughter continued heading straight for each other.

The DI mustered all her breath and might. "No!" she shouted. "Stop. Don't touch each other."

Father and daughter stopped running, turning towards the DI open-mouthed.

"What's going on?" Mills asked. "Maria?" he turned to his daughter. "Are you okay? I saw police and thought..."

"I'm fine, dad. What is going on? I thought something happened to you."

Yvonne held up her hands. "Just stay where you are, both of you, and I will explain."

Mills and his daughter had paused several metres from each other.

The DI triangulated with them. "I know how strange this must seem, but please bear with me and listen. We believe, Councillor Mills, someone exposed you to one part of a dangerous chemical mixture. We think they may have contaminated the door to your home with the other part." She looked at Maria. "I am sorry. We knocked, but there was no answer."

The girl took the headphones from around her neck. "Sorry, I was listening to this." She swallowed. "Are we in danger? Is this chemical harming me?"

Yvonne shook her head. "Not if you and your father do not touch. Each constituent on its own is harmless. They are only harmful when together. You must stay away from each other. No hugging... We have specialist officers coming who will test yourselves and the house for contamination. If we have this wrong, I apologise. But it is better to be safe than sorry."

"Is this what happened at the Eisteddfod?" Mills frowned.

"We believe it was," she answered. "I'm sorry to startle you both like that. But I assure you it was necessary."

Behind, she heard the approach of vehicles, and the sirens of ambulances. "This is the hazardous chemicals team who will swab and test your home. They will also instruct you on how to decontaminate safely if you have the chemicals on you. We may need your clothing and any swabs for evidence, if they test positive. Remember... don't touch each other."

HAZMAT-SUITED OFFICERS GOT to work swabbing and testing the exterior of the home, while others swabbed Mills and his daughter, before putting them both through a mobile decontamination unit comprising a multi-chambered trailer. The specialist unit contained a negative pressure filtration system, contaminated and clean separation rooms, and shower room.

Progress was slow and methodical, to ensure the safety of all involved at each stage.

Meanwhile, two officers were hard at work at the house, as Dewi and Yvonne paced up and down along the lane.

After what seemed like an age, one of the specialist officers who had taken off his mask approached the DI.

His actions surprised Yvonne. "Everything okay?" she asked.

"The house is clear," he answered, "and so is the girl. The gentleman was positive for the same chemical which was present at the council offices, but there was no evidence of contamination at the home. We checked the councillor's vehicle to make sure that was clear too."

The DI puffed her cheeks out, confused but relieved.

"There is no risk to the individuals or us, as things stand," he added. "We will bag the councillor's clothing for evidence, and he is being decontaminated as we speak. The girl was clean of the substances we tested for."

"Thank God." Yvonne nodded. "Thank you, to you and your staff, for your help."

THE DI and Dewi waited to speak to Kevin Mills about his meeting with Kamal Bronson.

Yvonne rubbed her chin, deep in thought. "Dewi, I don't get it..."

"Ma'am?"

"Why would Bronson risk Mills coming home and showering after the first exposure?"

"What are you thinking?" Dewi cocked his head. "I can see the cogs whirring..."

"Kamal has a meeting with the councillor and contaminates him with one part of a nerve agent. The obvious implication is he intended on exposing the councillor to the second contaminant at a later stage, right?"

"Yes..."

"Except, it isn't on the house or his vehicle."

"No."

"Well, how was the second exposure going to happen?"

They stared at each other, Yvonne's brow furrowing. "Bronson's here..."

Dewi shook his head. "If he was here, he'll have fled with all the activity going on."

"Not if he couldn't get away. Look at the road... It's full of police and other emergency service vehicles. He would not risk being seen. Come on..."

"Where are we going?"

"We're taking a little walk, right after I have requested an armed response backup."

20

CLEAR AND PRESENT DANGER

They walked up the lane in the opposite direction to the one they had used to arrive at the home.

"If he is around, then so is his vehicle." Yvonne swivelled her head around as they walked. "I bet he's watching from somewhere."

"I still think he'll be long gone." Dewi pushed both hands in his pockets, walking backwards to see how far they had come. "We shouldn't go much further until our backup arrives," he added.

"I hear you." She turned to him. "But remember, he cannot possibly have the active form of nerve agent with him. He could not deliver it when dead. So if he is here, the most he can have in his possession is the second constituent, which is harmless on its own. If he has other weapons, we might be in trouble. Otherwise, he has more to worry about than we do."

Dewi looked doubtful.

"Okay, okay..." The DI held up her hands. "We'll stop and wait for backup."

"Wait, what's that?" Dewi pointed to a gap in the hedge

ahead, where they could barely see the nose of a white vehicle. "Doesn't Bronson drive a white Tesla?"

"He does..." Yvonne quickened her step.

"Wait, let's think about this." Dewi paused.

The DI was now only a few feet from the car, craning her neck to see more of it. She jumped back. "It's a Tesla... It has Bronson's private plates."

"You are so observant. Clever girl." Kamal Bronson stepped out from behind the hedge.

Beyond him, and the reason he hadn't fled in his vehicle, were two parked police vans; one of them, a camera van. Unfortunately, neither looked occupied.

Yvonne had her eyes fixed firmly on Bronson's face.

He pulled a child's pump-action water pistol from behind his back. "Stay where you are," he instructed. "His eyes wandered to the vans, as he satisfied himself there was no-one in them." He held the water gun up, priming and pointing it at them. "You are going to let me go to my car and drive out of here."

Dewi raised both brows. "What are you going to do? Soak us to death?"

"You don't know what this is." Bronson sneered. "It's nerve agent."

The DI took a step towards him. "If that was nerve agent, Kamal, you would be a dead man."

He waved the plastic gun above his head. "This is just one part."

"Well, then it's harmless." The DI took another step, accompanied by Dewi. Sweat beaded on her temples, and on the small of her back.

"You don't understand..." Bronson displayed a smile that was pure evil. "I have already exposed you to the other part."

"What?" Yvonne paused mid-step.

"Oh, yes... You went to the council offices earlier, didn't you?"

"Yes, but we didn't touch anything."

"But you parked in the car park, right?"

The DI swallowed. "You don't know our car."

"Really? Do you mean it isn't the black BMW? The one you parked next to my Tesla when you came to my offices?"

Both detectives swallowed.

"Now, let me see... You are... what? Six or seven metres away? This can shoot up to twelve metres."

Yvonne's brain raced. Were they at risk? Had he really sprayed their car earlier that day? And, if there was any chemical on her and the DS, was it still capable of reacting? Wishing she knew more, she held her hands up in front of her. "Okay, don't spray." She and Dewi took a step back.

Kamal pulled a key fob out of his pocket. His Tesla beeped in response. "I'm going to drive out of here. I want you to stay right where you-"

Sirens blared as the armed response unit approached in the distance.

Bronson sprayed both Yvonne and Dewi and ran, jumping over the gate towards the woods at the back of Councillor Mills's house.

THE DI and Dewi coughed and spluttered as the liquid ran down their faces and soaked into their clothing, despite their desperate attempts to brush it off.

"I'm so sorry, Dewi," Yvonne said, wiping it from her face with her shirtsleeves.

The DS called over his radio to inform other officers they had been attacked, and that the suspect had run into the wood. He took his jacket off, using the inside to wipe his face. He offered it to Yvonne, who had not been wearing her jacket. "We should make our way back to the decontamination unit." He sounded calm, but the DI suspected his heart was racing as fast as hers.

"Yes..." Her eyes travelled towards the wood, where Bronson had disappeared. "I'm so sorry," she said again.

"Are you feeling anything?" Dewi shook his jacket.

"Not yet..." Yvonne raised her eyes to his. "Should we be in agony or something by now?"

"Well, if I remember correctly the footage I saw of the assassination in Kuala Lumpur airport, we should have felt the effects by now. The Korean dissident needed first aid within a couple of minutes."

"I am still not feeling anything."

"Me neither."

Yvonne looked towards the trees. "I think he lied to us, and I will not let him get away. Dewi, I would like you to make your way back. Paramedics are on their way, and you will get help sooner if I am wrong about this."

"What are you going to do?"

"Listen to my gut instinct and chase down our suspect."

"You don't think I am going to let you do that on your own, do you?"

"You have to, Dewi. I got us into this mess. It's my responsibility."

"Let's go." The DS set off running, quickly followed by the DI.

Behind them, shouts signalled the imminent arrival of their backup and ambulances.

21

THE HUNTER BECOMES THE HUNTED

The wooded landscape around Kerry comprised a rich summer tapestry of greens and browns. And the hills, textured with a soft downy grass, would normally have held their attention for a while. Instead, they barely noticed it as they worked their way into the wood, heads flicking back and forth; ears pricked and listening for movement. The high humidity weighed on them as they pursued the fleeing Kamal Bronson. The two detectives had become hunters stalking their prey, their brows beading perspiration.

Towering oaks and horse chestnut trees formed a dense canopy overhead, their leaves fluttering in the occasional breeze. The wood became a labyrinth of shadows, where dappled sunlight cast intricate patterns on the forest floor.

Yvonne paused, listening again, scratching her head as she spied crawlies moving amongst the detritus. To her right, Dewi moved with calculated precision, footsteps careful and silent, like a ghost amidst the ancient trees. They knew Kamal was close, and that he was capable of murder. They hoped to see him before he saw them.

Armed officers caught up with them, rustling through the long grass, and surrounding the wood where the fugitive was hiding.

Yvonne and Dewi crouched behind a gnarled oak. The DS exchanged a meaningful glance with the DI. They would have to make sure the approaching officers knew they were there. It wouldn't do to be caught up in live fire.

As armed police fanned out, Kamal Bronson went to ground. The brown tee shirt and camouflage cargo pants he wore would blend seamlessly with dark foliage. Yvonne and Dewi proceeded after exchanging hand signals with the leader of the armed officers. His wave reassured them he knew of their presence. They followed his men, staying alert.

As the sultry air sapped their energy, the detectives' shirts clung to their backs. Their eyes darted in all directions. There was no sign of Bronson.

The response team continued advancing, entering the trees and negotiating the undergrowth. A rustling of leaves and the murmur of voices punctured the air. The net was closing in on the killer. The forest, once serene, filled with hunched armour-clad figures, combing the ground tree by tree.

Yvonne and Dewi moved closer to where they believed Kamal was lying low, their movements deliberate and cautious. Each snapping twig sent adrenaline coursing through tired veins.

They approached a dense area where the undergrowth lay thick and unruly. Kamal could be hiding within it, and ready to strike at a moment's notice. Yvonne and Dewi watched as armed officers signalled to each other to split up and flank the thicket from the opposite side.

Their radios remained silent as they manoeuvred

through the woods, connected by an unspoken understanding. The trees closed in, eerie and claustrophobic. The tension was palpable, as though everything in the forest was holding its breath.

YVONNE CROUCHED, sure they had ventured far enough.

Dewi joined her as the two watched their armed colleagues continue the search. Neither wished to interfere with the response team, who had enough on their plate without needing to worry about accidentally harming officers from CID.

As exhaustion set in, Yvonne ruminated on the risks she had taken. Not only with her own safety, but that of her trusted sergeant. They were both fine, but it could so easily have been different if Kamal Bronson had been telling the truth about spraying their car.

Bronson had been lying in wait for Councillor Mills, intent on spraying the victim with the second constituent of the nerve agent as soon as he arrived home. The fact he intended delivering it with a water gun showed the callousness with which he was ready to act. To see the look in Mills's eyes as he delivered the death blow. The DI shuddered as she remembered the coldness in Bronson's stare when he aimed the plastic gun at her and Dewi. Her heart thudded so hard, she thought it would burst from her rib cage. She took reassurance from the fact they had spoiled his plans. Police vehicles, arriving from all directions, had caused the desperate Bronson to flee on foot until he thought the coast was clear. He would be an ominous threat to the community until caught.

A shout went up as Bronson sprang from his hiding

place amidst the trees. He ran, chased by several armed officers, their footfall muffled by undergrowth. The chase was on. Yvonne and Dewi exchanged glances, and without a word, joined the pursuit.

Bronson darted down a narrow forest path, followed by armed officers. The DI could hear their laboured breathing and the pounding of boots amidst the undergrowth. He was fast, but so were the officers chasing him, as they navigated the forest terrain with precision.

They emerged into a small forest clearing. A fallen tree had blocked Bronson's escape route. He skidded to a halt, desperation showing in the way he tossed his head, looking for a way out amidst the trees. Armed officers shouted at him to stay where he was, forming a tight circle, like trees in the forest.

"Kamal Bronson, you're surrounded by police," they announced, weapons aloft; their eyes watching him through gun sights. "There's no way out. Give up now, and you won't get hurt."

Bronson's gaze darted from one to another, panic etched on his face. He clutched the water pistol tightly and, for a moment, Yvonne feared he might use it, even though she knew it did not contain an active nerve agent. The pressure was all on the killer now, and he knew it.

Slowly, he lowered the makeshift weapon and raised his hands in surrender. "All right," he said, his voice shaky. "Please don't shoot."

Yvonne watched armed officers move in; cuffing him in the clearing. He said nothing as they arrested him on suspicion of murder and attempted murder, and marched him back towards the road. It was finally over.

As they led Bronson away through the trees, Yvonne felt a mixture of tiredness and relief. They had captured a dangerous killer, but she wondered what drove him to take the actions he had. The man appeared to have everything. What had made him risk it all and become a cold-blooded murderer?

There were still questions to answer but, for now, the immediate threat was gone. She could finally exhale, knowing that the town, Councillor Mills, and his family were safer tonight because of their actions.

They had been on a rollercoaster of emotions all day. The DI finally realised how tired she was.

Dewi put a reassuring hand on her shoulder. "Are you all right?" he asked, his gaze soft.

"I will be," she nodded. "I am so sorry I put you in danger, Dewi."

"Hey, you didn't. I made my own choices." He pressed his lips together. "Kamal Bronson won't be operating his dodgy business for a while." He tossed his head towards the figure being marched towards the police vehicles. "I'm only glad he is off the streets. I think he is one of the most dangerous individuals we have dealt with."

She nodded. "I'm inclined to agree." As they made their way back to their vehicle, Yvonne knew she would likely face questions from the DCI tonight or tomorrow, but all she wanted to do was sleep.

22

A PROPER DRESSING DOWN

Yvonne and Dewi arrived back at CID after decontamination. Callum made a brew and handed mugs to them both. "That was an amazing result... You must be exhausted. Maybe Llewelyn will give you a day or two as leave?"

The DI grimaced. "I took my eye off the ball. He may not be happy."

Callum shrugged. "Surely, what matters is you got the perp and stopped further attacks? Counter Terror has been in touch."

"Oh?" The DI cocked her head.

"Yeah... Apparently, Bronson was on their watch list for a few years. He joined a militant group while at college, where he was quite vocal. His organisation was behind offensive posters criticising immodest women, amongst other groups. The college had them taken down."

"You said for a few years, why did they stop watching him?" Yvonne sipped her tea.

"He led an apparently normal, law-abiding life until

now. He kept his nose clean for fifteen years after he left university."

"But he was obviously willing to harm others to get his own way?"

"Exactly... They attributed his previous behaviour to the folly of youth. They took him off the list, not realising the potential for harm was still there."

Dewi yawned. "I shall sleep like a log tonight. I feel like I've run a marathon."

The DI grinned. "I think we actually did... We must have covered at least a couple of miles hunting Bronson."

"I must admit, when he sprayed us with that gun-thing, I almost crapped my pants." Dewi pulled a face. "He definitely had me there."

The DI put down her mug. "I can't believe I put you in that situation." She ran a hand through straggled hair, her brow furrowed. "What was I thinking?"

"Hey... I put myself in that situation. You wanted me to go back down the lane to meet paramedics, remember?"

"Sure, but I should have known you would follow me. It could have ended so differently." Yvonne's stomach knotted. This sinking feeling was not what usually followed a successful takedown of a violent perpetrator. "I took my eye off the ball."

"You beat the big boys with his capture, Yvonne." Dai joined them, his gaze empathetic. "When they phoned us to inform of Bronson's history, you were already chasing him through the woods."

"I'm glad he's in custody." The DI leaned against her desk, holding the mug in both hands, her blue eyes soulful.

DCI Llewelyn came into the main office, his shirt sleeves rolled up. "Congratulations to all of you. Good to know the park attacker is cooling his heels in custody." The smile he would usually have sported at such times was notably absent. His eyes travelled toward Yvonne. "Can I have a word?"

The DI swallowed, placing down her mug. "Sure..." She followed him to his office.

He shut the door. "Please take a seat."

She did as she was told, lips pursed.

He sat behind his desk, the coolness in his voice a warning of what was to come. "I'm torn," he began. "I am obviously pleased we have Bronson in the cells and glad the town is safer today than it was yesterday. But I am not happy with the risks you took to make this happen."

"I'm sorry, I-"

He held up his hand, stopping her mid-sentence. "I know we've been here before, and I arguably should have taken greater action when you got yourself shot up a couple of years ago. It is to both our detriment that I did not. I thought your injuries, and the ordeal you had suffered, would have been enough to stop you from being reckless in the future. Looks like I was wrong."

She pressed her lips together. He really was angry with her.

He continued. "This time, however, you put not only yourself in harm's way, you also took Dewi into a risky situation in which a perpetrator could have killed you both." He sighed. "What do you have to say for yourself?"

Her gaze moved to the window, and the top branches of an ash tree fluttering in the breeze. "I'm sorry... I realise what we did was crazy. It's no excuse, but I was terrified Bronson would get away. He was desperate, and capable of doing desperate things." The DI could have informed Llewelyn that she told Dewi to go back, and not to follow her, but that wasn't in her nature. Yvonne wasn't one to abrogate responsibility, under any circumstances. The fault must lie squarely on her shoulders where it belonged.

"What were you thinking? You suspected the man of using a nerve agent. He had already killed two people and injured many others. Why did you not wait for backup? Why risk him exposing you and Dewi to extreme danger? Dewi has a family, and you have a partner. What would they have done without you? What would we have done?"

"It's not really an excuse, but it was a calculated risk. I knew he couldn't be holding an active nerve agent in that water pistol, because he himself would have been dead. What I didn't expect was that he might have already sprayed our vehicle earlier. I hadn't factored that in. I was genuinely shocked and horrified when he said he had done that. He lied, thankfully. But that was the first time I felt terror at our situation."

"So why cause him to use the spray?"

"We didn't... Not exactly, anyway. The sirens from the ARV spooked him. I think he sprayed in order to shock us and stop us from following him into the wood. He hoped we would be more interested in getting help than in stopping him from escaping. And for a minute, he was right. But when we realised there were no after-effects when there should have been, we followed him until armed officers caught up. I didn't want us losing him... Not while he had that chemical on him, at least."

"What you should have done was ensure yourself and Dewi got back down to paramedics, and the decontamination unit. Just because you hadn't yet succumbed to anything, that didn't mean there wasn't a delayed response to the chemical. You couldn't be sure what he showered you with. And poisons are more effective in the nose and mouth than they are on the skin. It might still kill you, but it's slower acting on the skin."

"I understand, sir, and I take full responsibility for my actions. I simply assumed if he had a nerve agent in that toy, which would have been dripping on him, he would be ill or dead. We knew he had already used the first reagent that morning to spray the councillor's office. I believed he would have showered and changed before taking the second to finish the councillor off, and I assumed we would be safe. I own that, now with hindsight, I was utterly reckless and should have acted differently."

"You know this could be a disciplinary matter, right?"

She nodded, her eyes dropping to the floor. "I do."

"Go home. Get some rest. Think about things."

"Thank you, sir."

"Don't come back for a few days."

"Sir?"

"I need to think, and perhaps discuss matters with the superintendent. We may suspend you pending any hearing. I'm sorry, Yvonne."

"Don't be... I did this to myself."

As she left the DCI's office, all she really wanted was to be home with Tasha. Hot tears fell from her lashes, which she brushed away with the back of her hand. It was time to go home.

A TIRED, red-eyed Yvonne arrived home that evening defeated, a feeling she was unused to after successfully concluding a tough case.

Tasha sensed something was wrong and approached

from the lounge, taking the DI's coat to hang it up. "Are you okay?"

"I will be..." The DI nodded. "I'm tired, and in need of a hug."

The psychologist did not wait to be asked twice. She pulled her partner into her arms and swayed her for a while. No need for words. Yvonne rested her head on the psychologist's shoulder.

"Want to talk about it?" Tasha asked, finally.

"I don't know... I might be in trouble with you as well, if I do?"

"Never." Tasha grinned.

Yvonne pulled back to look at her partner. "Really?"

The psychologist pulled a face. "Depends what you've done."

"See? I knew it." Yvonne laughed through watery emotional eyes. "Maybe, after dinner..."

"No problem." Tasha moved towards the kitchen. "You get showered and changed, and we'll discuss it after tea."

"So, go on... What's bugging you? What have you been up to? No doubt it's related to this case you've been working on?" Tasha handed a glass of cold chardonnay to Yvonne as they sat on floor cushions, a bay window partially open allowing in a cool evening breeze.

Yvonne explained what had gone on that day, and how it related to their case. When she got to the spraying incident, the psychologist spat out a mouthful of wine. "He did what?" She brushed her shirt with her hand.

"He sprayed us both and took off into the wood. Sirens

were blaring, and Dewi and I stood there dripping; looking at each other, wondering if we were about to drop."

"Bloody hell, Yvonne..."

"See? It has to be bad if it makes even you swear..." The DI puffed out her cheeks. "Boy, am I in trouble."

"Well, he could have killed you."

"Don't I know it? And, worse, I could have caused Dewi to be killed alongside me. It's a total crap-fest, isn't it?"

Tasha pursed her lips. "So, he hadn't really sprayed your car, then?"

"Well, no... He only said that to stop us arresting him. I think he knew the game was up. He had probably known days before, but kept going anyway. I suspect he felt he had nothing left to lose. He would have killed the councillor, without our timely intervention. Perhaps, his last hoorah?"

"But he could also have finished you..." Tasha ran both hands through her hair. "And I knew nothing of what was going on."

"It's a good job, or you would probably have been there, too. There would have been three of us dripping chemicals; wondering if our chips were up."

The psychologist smiled. "You're a silly sod, you know that?"

"Yes."

"So, what happens now?"

Yvonne shrugged. "I don't know... A disciplinary hearing? The DCI intimated that was his intention."

"I see..."

"I could lose my job, Tasha."

"You won't lose your job."

"You think?"

"You are brilliant at what you do, and you are successful

at catching serious offenders. They would bite off their own nose to spite their face if they let you go."

"Oh, good."

"You could get demoted, though."

"I knew it."

"DC Yvonne Giles... It has a certain ring to it..."

Yvonne laughed, giving her partner a gentle push. "Stop taking the micky." She grinned. "This is serious." Her brow furrowed. "Mind you, you may have a point. What if they do?"

"What? Demote you?"

"Yes... I'd have to make the tea. Stop laughing. That really would be serious."

"I'm glad you seem a little better." Tasha held up her wine. "To you, Yvonne. And to the successful conclusion of your case. Whatever the outcome of any hearing, you have helped put a dangerous killer behind bars. And that means everything."

"Thanks." Yvonne settled back to finish her glass.

23

A TIME TO CONSIDER

T he DI knocked on Jonathan Tudor's door and waited. Eyes on the street, she watched people coming and going; the neighbourhood moving on, following the loss of one of its own.

"Yes?"

She spun round to find Tudor in the doorway, his red eyes sporting large bags underneath. "Hello, Mr Tudor. I came to give you the news about your wife's killer."

"Oh..." He looked surprised at that, as though he had expected her to question him and his movements again. "I didn't know you'd caught anyone."

"We arrested someone yesterday afternoon. It will hit the headlines later today, but I wanted to tell you in person."

"Well, you'd better come in." He held the door open, allowing her to walk ahead of him. "You had best go into the kitchen. The kids are in the lounge."

She cast a glance towards the children, who were busy building something with Lego. "I'm glad to see them playing. They seem happier."

"They are getting there. They still have moments, and

they will for a while, but now they have longer periods when they forget the hurt."

She nodded, taking a seat at the pine kitchen table, her eyes travelling over the plain white cupboards. "I also wanted to apologise to you..."

"For what?" He frowned.

"For suspecting you, and questioning you at such an upsetting time. It is one of the hardest parts of my job, treating victims' partners and friends as suspects for their murder. It sometimes feels like I am victimising people all over again."

He sighed. "It's frustrating," he said, "but I understand it's your job. And I know statistics suggest a partner is often involved in a murder. I get it. It didn't make it easier to bear, though. I really did and still do, love my wife. And I miss her. I slept very little last night."

"It shows... I'm so sorry."

"I lay thinking of her the whole time, wondering what I could have done differently that day. If only we hadn't gone to the Eisteddfod..."

"You mustn't punish yourself. Any other time, it would have been a memorable day out that you would have looked back on fondly for years..."

"You said you arrested someone?"

"We did, an entrepreneur. He is in custody. I cannot give too many details right now, but there will be a press conference later today given by DCI Llewelyn. It's going to be televised if you cannot be there in person."

He grimaced. "I can't go... The children..."

"I wanted to ask you about that." She cocked her head. "Just as I would ask you to forgive us for suspecting you, I would ask that you consider forgiving Charmaine. She loved her sister and adores your children. I know she is more than willing to help you with them any time you need. She would babysit them for you. I know you were angry that she blamed you for Charlene's death because of the affair, but she was hurting... as you were, too. Can you not find it in your heart to forgive her? I suspect Emily and David would love spending more time with their aunt. And they need a female figure right now."

As though hearing their names, the two children appeared in the doorway, eight-year-old Emily holding a rag doll.

"Hello, you... What's your dolly's name?" the DI asked.

"She's called Amanda Jane." The girl gave a broad smile. "She is three years old." Her face became more serious. "Are you here to talk about mummy?"

The DI lifted her gaze to the girl's father, who nodded assent. "Yes, Emily, I am," she answered.

"Mummy is watching us from Heaven," Emily asserted, wide-eyed.

Yvonne smiled. "Yes, she is."

"And she's watching Amanda Jane, too."

"Most certainly." Tears pricked the DI's eyes. She fought them back.

"Is mummy watching me, too?" David asked.

"Most definitely, and she is so proud and pleased with both of you. She couldn't be prouder. And she knows when you are being good for your daddy."

The children smiled, though there was a seriousness in their eyes.

The DI felt their pain. "I'd better be going..." She rose from her seat. "I wish you the very best in the future, and we will keep you informed as regards the prosecution. Victim liaison will be there to support you if needed," she said to Jonathan.

"Thank you." He held out his hand for her to shake. "And thank you for catching my wife's-" He stopped himself, looking down at the children, and shrugged. "You know..."

"Yes..." Yvonne nodded. "I'll see myself out."

SAM HARRIES WAS out of hospital, and enjoying a cup of tea on the deck in front of his bungalow. He waved to her as she approached the garden gate. "Hello officer."

"Hello." She grinned at his demotion of her rank. Was this a portent? "How are you, Mr Harries?"

"I am much better, thank you," he answered. Sam had a woollen blanket over his knees as he sat enjoying a mug of tea; watching the world go by.

"I came to check on you." Yvonne smiled. "The last time I saw you, you were looking rather peaky on the hospital ward."

"Yes, I had quite a scare."

"How long have you been out of the hospital?"

"Nearly a week." He made as though to get up. "Would you like a cup of tea?"

She held up a hand. "No, thank you, Mr Harries. I had one recently. I came to let you know that we have arrested someone for the contamination at the park."

"Oh, good... Oh, that is good news." He placed the blanket back over his knees. "I was wondering, as I had heard nothing."

"There's a press conference later today. It will be on the news."

"I shall look out for it." He nodded. "You've done a good job catching the person. I'm very impressed."

The DI wished everyone felt that way. She thought of

the DCI, and the fact she was on enforced leave for a few days while he decided her fate. She was visiting victims on her own time, but it was what she wanted.

"Are you sure you don't want to join me for a cuppa?" Sam tilted his head.

She glanced around, realising for the first time that he was probably lonely. Sam's bungalow on the Milford Road in Newtown stood detached, with no neighbours in sight, even though it was one among several on the same hill. "Sure, why not?" She smiled. "I'll make it. Would you like another?"

The DI whiled away an hour with the older man, listening to him recount tales of his youth, and of his wife who had passed away two years earlier from cancer. She felt better for listening to someone else's story. It helped put things into perspective.

As Yvonne left, both of them felt a little brighter than when she arrived.

~

A GENTLE SEA shimmered in the late summer sun. It licked her toes, the cool water sucking the tension from out of them; calming frayed nerves.

Yvonne lingered, eyes closed, taking in a large lungful of salty air, face turned to the sun.

"They used to recommend it for people living with tuberculosis, you know." Tasha watched her partner, understanding the DI's need for quietude.

"I can see why..." Yvonne opened one eye, turning her gaze to the psychologist. "This was a good idea of yours."

Her fiancé grinned, sunlight glinting in her chocolate

hair. "Thought you could do with a weekend away from it all; help you put things into perspective."

"I refuse to feel sorry for myself, Tasha." The DI pushed her hands deep into the pockets of her shorts, looking more relaxed in a short-sleeved, white cotton shirt. "Que sera, sera."

"You're quoting lyrics at me. I'm getting worried. You'll be singing, next."

"Shall we go in?" Yvonne walked further into the water.

The psychologist looked down at the jeans she had rolled up, but couldn't quite get over her knees, and pulled a face. "I don't fancy eating lunch wearing wet things... sorry, I don't mean to be a spoilsport. I can watch you though, and live vicariously."

"We could run away..." Yvonne splashed about in the surf.

"Are you that worried about your meeting with the DCI next week?"

"Maybe?"

"For what it's worth, I think you're worrying for nothing. I told you, I don't want to tempt fate, but I believe there is no way your superiors would let you go." Tasha dipped her toes in the water.

Yvonne was already up to her thighs. "I'm fine; I'm a big girl."

"Good... Otherwise, I'd have to tell you all over again what a brilliant and hard-working detective you are, and I am running out of ways to say it. You make mistakes... You're human. We all do it. Don't think," Tasha ordered, "just feel." Against her better judgement, the psychologist went for it — running through the surf to join her partner. The thighs of her jeans were now drenched.

Yvonne laughed. "Uh oh, you'll have to eat lunch in your knickers."

The psychologist grimaced. "Don't joke, this water is freezing, I might have to..."

Later, they tucked into scampi and a cheeky glass of white at Rummers Wine Bar near Aberystwyth harbour. And planned their afternoon and evening, having already booked a room at their favourite B&B, also on the harbour.

"Thank you, Tasha." Yvonne smiled, her hand on her partner's. "Thank you for being there, and for helping me feel better. I'll talk to the DCI. It will all work out in the wash. I will grovel profusely, and promise to be even more safety conscious in the future."

Tasha raised a brow. "But will you mean it?"

"Of course."

∾

AFTERWORD

Watch out for Book 22 in the DI Giles Series, coming soon...

Stick around until the end of this book for a special treat: The first chapter of 'Murder on Arthur's Seat' the first book in my brand new series - The DI McKenzie Series.

Mailing list: You can join my emailing list here : AnnamarieMorgan.com
  Facebook page: AnnamarieMorganAuthor

You might also like to read the other books in the DI Giles Series:

Book 1: Death Master:

After months of mental and physical therapy, Yvonne Giles, an Oxford DI, is back at work and that's just how she likes it. So when she's asked to hunt the serial killer responsible for taking apart young women, the DI jumps at the chance but hides the fact she is suffering debilitating flashbacks. She is told to work with Tasha Phillips, an in-her-face, criminal psychologist. The DI is not enamoured with the idea. Tasha has a lot to prove. Yvonne has a lot to get over. A tentative link with a 20 year-old cold case brings them closer to the truth but events then take a horrifyingly personal turn.

Book 2: You Will Die

After apprehending an Oxford Serial Killer, and almost losing her life in the process, DI Yvonne Giles has left England for a quieter life in rural Wales.Her peace is shattered when she is asked to hunt a priest-killing psychopath, who taunts the police with messages inscribed on the corpses.Yvonne requests the help of Dr. Tasha Phillips, a psychologist and friend, to aid in the hunt. But the killer is one step ahead and the ultimatum, he sets them, could leave everyone devastated.

Book 3: Total Wipeout

A whole family is wiped out with a shotgun. At first glance, it's an open-and-shut case. The dad did it, then killed himself. The deaths follow at least two similar family wipeouts – attributed to the financial crash.

So why doesn't that sit right with Detective Inspector Yvonne Giles? And why has a rape occurred in the area, in the weeks preceding each family's demise? Her seniors do not believe there are questions to answer. DI Giles must therefore risk everything, in a high-stakes investigation ofa mysterious masonic ring and players in high finance.

Can she find the answers, before the next innocent family is wiped out?

Book 4: Deep Cut

In a tiny hamlet in North Wales, a female recruit is murdered whilst on Christmas home leave. Detective Inspector Yvonne Giles is asked to cut short her own leave, to investigate. Why was the young soldier killed? And is her death related to several alleged suicides at her army base? DI Giles this it is, and that someone powerful has a dark secret they will do anything to hide.

Book 5: The Pusher

Young men are turning up dead on the banks of the River Severn. Some of them have been missing for days or even weeks. The only thing the police can be sure of, is that the men have drowned. Rumours abound that a mythical serial killer has turned his attention from the Manchester canal to the waterways of Mid-Wales. And now one of CID's own is missing. A brand new recruit with everything to live for. DI Giles must find him before it's too late.

Book 6: Gone

Children are going missing. They are not heard from again until sinister requests for cryptocurrency go viral. The public must pay or the children die. For lead detective Yvonne Giles, the case is complicated enough. And then the unthinkable happens...

Book 7: Bone Dancer

A serial killer is murdering women, threading their bones back together, and leaving them for police to find. Detective Inspector Yvonne Giles must find him before more innocent victims die. Problem is, the killer wants her and will do anything he can to get her. Unaware that she, herself, is is a target, DI Giles risks everything to catch him.

Book 8: Blood Lost

A young man comes home to find his whole family missing. Half-eaten breakfasts and blood spatter on the lounge wall are the only clues to what happened...

Book 9: Angel of Death

The peace of the Mid-Wales countryside is shattered, when a female eco-warrior is found crucified in a public wood. At first, it would appear a simple case of finding which of the woman's enemies had had her killed. But DI Yvonne Giles has no idea how bad things are going to get. As the body count rises, she will need all of her instincts, and the skills of those closest to her, to stop the murderous rampage of the Angel of Death.

Book 10: Death in the Air

Several fatal air collisions have occurred within a few months in rural Wales. According to the local Air Accidents Investigation Branch (AAIB) inspector, it's a coincidence. Clusters happen. Except, this cluster is different. DI Yvonne Giles suspects it when she hears some of the witness statements but, when an AAIB inspector is found dead under a bridge, she knows it.

Something is way off. Yvonne is determined to get to the bottom of the mystery, but exactly how far down the treacherous rabbit hole is she prepared to go?

Book 11: Death in the Mist

The morning after a viscous sea-mist covers the seaside town of Aberystwyth, a young student lies brutalised within one hundred yards of the castle ruins.

DI Yvonne Giles' reputation precedes her. Having successfully captured more serial killers than some detectives have caught colds, she is seconded to head the murder investigation team, and hunt down the young woman's killer.

What she doesn't know, is this is only the beginning...

Book 12: Death under Hypnosis

When the secretive and mysterious Sheila Winters approaches Yvonne Giles and tells her that she murdered someone thirty years before, she has the DI's immediate attention.

Things get even more strange when Sheila states:

She doesn't know who.

She doesn't know where.

She doesn't know why.

Book 13: Fatal Turn

A seasoned hiker goes missing from the Dolfor Moors after recording a social media video describing a narrow cave he intends to explore. A tragic accident? Nothing to see here, until a team of cavers disappear on a coastal potholing expedition, setting off a string of events that has DI Giles tearing her hair out. What, or who is the thread that ties this series of disappearances together?

A serial killer, thriller murder-mystery set in Wales.

Book 14: The Edinburgh Murders

A newly-retired detective from the Met is murdered in a murky alley in Edinburgh, a sinister calling card left with the body.

The dead man had been a close friend of psychologist Tasha Phillips, giving her her first gig with the Met decades before.

Tasha begs DI Yvonne Giles to aid the Scottish police in solving the case.

In unfamiliar territory, and with a ruthless killer haunting the streets, the DI plunges herself into one of the darkest, most terrifying cases of her career. Who exactly is The Poet?

Book 15: A Picture of Murder

Men are being thrown to their deaths in rural Wales.

At first glance, the murders appear unconnected until DI Giles uncovers potential links with a cold case from the turn of the Millennium.

Someone is eliminating the witnesses to a double murder.

DI Giles and her team must find the perpetrator before all the witnesses are dead.

Book 16: The Wilderness Murders

People are disappearing from remote locations.

Abandoned cars, neatly piled belongings, and bizarre last photographs, are the only clues for what happened to them.

Did they run away? Or, as DI Giles suspects, have they fallen prey to a serial killer who is taunting police with the heinous pieces of a puzzle they must solve if they are to stop the wilderness murderer.

Book 17: The Bunker Murders

A murder victim found in a shallow grave has DI Yvonne Giles and her team on the hunt for both the killer and a motive for the well-loved man's demise.

Yvonne cannot help feeling the killing is linked to a

string of female disappearances stretching back nearly two decades.

Someone has all the answers, and the DI will stop at nothing to find them and get to the bottom of this perplexing mystery.

Book 18: The Garthmyl Murders

A missing brother and friends with dark secrets have DI Giles turning circles after a body is found face-down in the pond of a local landmark.

Stymied by a wall of silence and superstition, Yvonne and her team must dig deeper than ever if they are to crack this impossible case.

Who, or what, is responsible for the Garthmyl murders?

Book 19: The Signature

When a young woman is found dead inside a rubbish dumpster after a night out, police chiefs are quick to label it a tragic accident. But as more bodies surface, Detective Inspector Yvonne Giles is convinced a cold-blooded murderer is on the loose. She believes the perpetrator is devious and elusive, disabling CCTV cameras in the area, and leaving them with little to go on. With time running out, Giles and her team must race against the clock to catch the killer or killers before they strike again.

Book 20: The Incendiary Murders

When the Powys mansion belonging to an ageing rock star is rocked by a deadly explosion, Detective Inspector Yvonne Giles finds herself tasked with a case of murder, suspicion, and secrets. As shockwaves ripple through the community, Giles must pierce the impenetrable facades of the characters surrounding the case, racing the clock to find the culprit and prevent further bombings. With an investigation full of twists and turns, DI Yvonne Giles must unravel the truth before it's too late.

Book 21 - The Park Murders

When two people are left dead and four others are seriously ill in hospital after a visit to a local nature park in rural Wales, DI Giles and her team find themselves in a race against time to stop a killer or killers hell-bent on terrorising the community. As the investigation deepens, the team must draw on all of their skill and experience to hunt down the elusive Powys poisoner before more lives are lost.

Remember to watch out for Book 22 in the DI Giles Series, coming soon...

The DI McKenzie Series

Book 1 - Murder on Arthur's seat. (Release date 15th December, 2023)

Chapter 1 - Taken

Gordon stood at the bar of The Last Drop tavern in Edinburgh's Old Town, feeling relaxed.

The pub was his sort of place; a respite from the outside world, where he could relax amid historic walls and modern-day comfort, and enjoy a traditional ale or a craft beer with good friends. Dark wooden tables and high-backed chairs invited patrons to settle in for a leisurely drink or a hearty meal. Adorned with old photographs and memorabilia, the walls offered a glimpse into Edinburgh's past and the pub's intriguing history. Dim lighting provided the escape from reality he craved, while the mixed scents of traditional Scottish dishes such as haggis, neeps, and tatties, and fish and chips filtered from the restaurant, reminding him of a childhood at his grandparent's croft. The tavern's ambience was homely and inviting; a haven where anxieties melted away and conversation thrived, even if it deteriorated into a drunken blether by the end of the night.

He looked across at Shania, her long blonde hair in a single plait like fancy French bread. Gordon thought it odd she would choose to spend her night off drinking at her workplace. But he was glad she did. He preferred her on this side of the bar. There were no barriers this way. She had her back to him, allowing his gaze to wander her elegant neck as he agonised over asking her out, something he felt he must do before starting a marine biology course at Edinburgh University in the autumn. Language was easy until butterflies invaded your stomach. Then, it became an incomprehensible mess. At least, it did for him.

It was his round and, as he handed over two crisp banknotes to the bartender, he signalled to his friends for help to get the drinks to their table.

After a short debate, Gordon's best mate was the chosen helper. Jock, dark-haired and gangly, was almost a foot taller than his friend. It brought out his protective instinct. The two of them, several packs of nuts between their teeth, carried six pints and a whiskey-coke over to the others.

"So, are you going to do it, then?" Jock asked, as they plonked the pints in front of thirsty friends.

"I don't know... I want to, it's just..."

"Just what? Look at her. She's over there waiting."

Gordon snuck another glance. "No, she's not... She's not even looking."

"Aye, but she was a wee while earlier. You know it. Come on, it's now or never. You'll be too busy to bother once your course starts. You'll miss your chance if you don't try now. Old golden chops over there will get to her first," Jock gestured to their fair-haired, handsome friend, Ben. Broad, with a shirt that stressed gym-going biceps, Ben was the one with a reputation for the girls.

Gordon grimaced. "Och, thanks, mate... That's all I need. Jings, he better not go over there, eh?"

"Well, go do it then." Jock gestured again with his head. "Talk to her."

"Aye, I'll need a smoke first. I need to work up to it."

"Well, don't leave it too long, eh?"

Gordon pulled a pack of cigarettes from his pocket and headed through the door onto the street. Heart pumping hard, it took three attempts to light the cigarette. His hands trembled too much. "Look at the state of me," he said aloud. "She'll not want to see me if I'm shaking like this."

The screech of brakes and tyres scraping along the road shocked him out of his reverie. He had no time to react.

Three men in balaclavas and dark clothing clambered out of a dark SUV with tinted windows. They grabbed Gordon while his mouth fell open, forcing a cloth bag over his head.

As the SUV sped away, the virgin cigarette burned red in the gutter where it had fallen.

Inside the pub, Jock checked his watch. Gordon had been gone for over twenty minutes. That wasn't like him. There was serious frost developing outside, and Goose wasn't one to be standing out in the cold for long. In fact, Gordon's nickname came about because of the pimpled flesh he broke out in at the mere mention of chill weather.

It didn't take this long to drum up the courage to speak to a lassie. Joch strode to the door of The Last Drop to check on his friend.

As the cold air stung his cheeks, he looked both ways

along the street. His mate was nowhere to be seen. "Gordon?" he called. "Goose?" Frowning, he returned to their friends.

"Where's Gord?" Mikey Munro asked, eyebrows raised.

Joch shrugged. "He said he was going for a smoke, but I can't find him. He's not outside, I looked."

"I'll check the bog. I need to go, anyway." Mikey got up. "He's probably making himself pretty for Shania over there..."

Joch laughed, but his eyes didn't crease. Something was up. He knew it.

Saturday morning, and Grant McKenzie was home with his family in one of The Grange's smaller Victorian properties, amongst the leafy suburbs south of Edinburgh city centre. All were still in their pyjamas.

The DI was puffing hard from running round the lounge playing aeroplanes with six-year-old Craig on his back and four-year-old Martha hugging his leg, both her tiny feet on one of his large ones.

Ten-year-old Davie gave them a stern look and a sigh. Considering himself far too old for such silly games, he pulled a face, unable to hear the cartoon he was watching.

"I'm hungry," Craig complained, as his dad dropped him onto the carpet.

"Me too." Martha rubbed her eyes. "And I'm thirsty."

"Aye, well, your mammy will have breakfast on the table in just a few minutes. Why don't you two go wash your hands and face? By the time you finish, your food will be ready."

As the younger children left to do as he asked, the phone rang.

He could hear the panic in his sister's voice, and the tremulous, breathless way she delivered clipped sentences.

"Gordon is missing... He's missing. Grant, my boy didn't come home last night, and his friends can't find him."

"Woah, Davina, slow down, hen. What do you mean his friends couldn't find him? He's a young lad. Maybe he stayed with a lassie?"

"You don't understand. He went outside to smoke, and didn't come back."

"What, at your house?"

"No, no, the pub. He was with friends at The Last Drop. They said he popped outside for a smoke, and never came back. Jock and the others looked for him everywhere. They said he vanished. Grant, I'm scared. Something's wrong."

The DI's heart pumped hard in his chest. He cleared his throat, keeping his voice calm and measured. "Davina, try not to worry. I'll get looking for him right away. Have you called the station?"

"Yes, I did, but they said they couldn't do anything until he's been missing for at least twenty-four hours."

"I'll handle it. Don't worry. I'll be there soon," Grant assured her, hanging up the phone. He headed for the kitchen to let his wife, Jane, know he had to leave.

Printed in Great Britain
by Amazon

30315209R00101